Dark Moon

A Decorah Security Novel

By Rebecca York

Ruth Glick writing as Rebecca York

Published by Light Street Press
Copyright © 2012 by Ruth Glick
Cover design by Patricia Rosemoor

ISBN: 978-0-9706293-9-5.

CHAPTER ONE

Her head was a little fuzzy, but that was okay. She didn't have to work tomorrow. Really, she didn't have to work at all, but she liked puttering around the little boutique on Charles Street that Daddy had bought her. It was fun having something of her own. Having employees and customers who liked the whimsical clothing and jewelry she brought back from New Delhi and Bangkok.

Tonight she only had to make it from the club to her apartment. She could have gone home with Craig, or one of the guys she'd flirted with on the dance floor. But she didn't like him enough to fall into his bed.

The din inside Temptation faded as she wove her way to the parking lot. With a sigh of relief, she reached her Beemer and clicked the button to unlock.

Before she could open the door, someone grabbed her from behind and covered her mouth with his hand. When she tried to pull away, he caught a fistful of her hair and yanked her head back, almost snapping her neck.

"Careful, you idiot," a rough voice cautioned. "She's a valuable commodity."

"Yeah."

The pressure on her neck eased as someone shoved her into the backseat of the Beemer and lifted the key from her hand.

1

The second guy climbed behind the wheel while the first one held her in place.

"Please," she whimpered as the car headed away from the club. "My father will pay to get me back."

The guy up front laughed. "Yeah. We know, sweetheart."

The kidnapper in back pressed something wet over her nose and mouth, and blackness closed in.

The phone jerked Emma Richards awake at 5:00 a.m.

The harsh voice on the other end of the line said, "We've got a priority job. I'm assembling a team. Get in here ASAP."

It was her boss, Frank Decorah, a tough former Navy Seal who had worked for a couple of top security companies before going into business for himself.

Instantly alert, she climbed out of bed and headed for a quick shower, then gave her medium-length blond hair two minutes with the hair dryer. Good enough.

The jeans she'd discarded before her three-mile jog around the lake were lying over the arm of a chair where she'd tossed them. A white blouse hung in the closet along with a tweed blazer.

No time for makeup. Not when something urgent was going down. But she knew better than to ask about the assignment until she was inside the Beltsville headquarters of Decorah Security. It was in an unpretentious warehouse area off Route One, convenient to both DC and Baltimore.

She pulled into a parking space beside the windowless building and hurried through the bland reception area. Once she'd punched in her code and entered the back of the building, everything changed to high tech efficiency.

She'd been with the company for five years, ever since she'd turned down an offer from her dad's security outfit in order to prove she could stand on her own two feet. So far she'd done pretty well, starting with routine surveillance

2

assignments and graduating to sophisticated sting operations and hair-trigger search and rescue.

She'd been happy at Decorah, until Cole Marshall had come on board last year. Frank Decorah had been enthusiastic about getting him. Emma wasn't quite so sure. There was something strange about the guy. Something she simply didn't understand and didn't trust. It wasn't just that he never socialized with the rest of the Decorah team. She had sensed an invisible barrier around him, a barrier nobody dared step through except Frank.

None of that stopped her from being attracted to him—an attraction she'd fought because she'd sensed that if she got involved with this man, it would be a lot more than a casual affair. And that frightened her in ways she couldn't explain.

She and Frank met in the hallway, his gait less steady than usual. Most days you wouldn't know that one of his legs was artificial. This morning he looked like he was in pain.

"Thanks for getting here so fast," he said. Another anomaly. It wasn't like him to thank his staff for reporting to work, all of which made her think that he was on edge over the upcoming job.

The moment she followed him into the conference room, her own nerves started to jangle.

Cole Marshall was sitting on the other side of the polished rosewood table.

Dark hair. Dark eyes. Dark tee shirt. He always reminded her of a predator on the hunt, which was probably why he made her nervous. They'd partnered on a few assignments, and she'd wanted to tell Decorah no way in hell would she do it again. But she knew that the boss understood the strengths of his staff and put the best team together for every job. This morning, it appeared that the outside operatives would be her and Cole.

He gave her a tight nod, indicating that he wasn't any happier to see her than she was to see him.

Teddy Granada came rushing in.

3

"Sorry I'm late."

Decorah gave him a stern look but said nothing because they all knew they were lucky to have the computer geek.

Teddy's name came from his appearance. He was six feet tall with the bulk of a grizzly. This morning he wore a wrinkled plaid shirt with a rip in the sleeve.

His cohort in the division, Stinger Henderson, rocked back and forth in his swivel chair like it was part of an amusement park ride. The polar opposite of Teddy, he looked like a refugee from a biker gang complete with leather jacket and boots. Under the jacket was an impressive set of tattoos, mostly of the horror movie variety.

Teddy and Stinger would be working from headquarters. While she and Cole would be doing what?

"What have we got?" Stinger asked as he bit at a hangnail.

Frank Decorah passed out folders with photos and background information. The photos showed a young woman with striking strawberry-colored hair and blue eyes.

Emma gasped when she saw the picture. "It's Karen Hopewell."

"You know her?" Frank asked sharply.

"We both went to Carlton Academy. She was a few years behind me. What happened to her?"

She failed to come home last night, and her dad is worried sick. Her mom died last year, and she's all he's got."

"Maybe she bunked with a friend," Teddy said.

"Possible, but unlikely. Considering that the father got a ransom demand early this morning."

Emma's stomach was churning as she took in the information. Someone she knew. Kidnapped.

Frank went on to give a few particulars. "She's the daughter of Morton Hopewell. Twenty-two years old. Dad set her up with a boutique on Charles Street after she graduated from the University of Maryland—with a major in partying."

He paused. "You can get more background from the briefing folders. The main point is that the kidnappers want five million dollars. If they don't get it in the next few days, Karen's life as she knew it ends, and they've said that if Hopewell contacts the cops, he'll be sorry."

Stinger's feet hit the floor as he abruptly stopped rocking. "They're going to off her?" he asked in his flat, matter-of-fact voice.

"The implication is that she'll wish she were dead," Frank answered in a voice that could have turned water to ice.

Emma winced, her imagination running wild as she thought about what the wrong kind of men could do to a twenty-two-year-old female.

"Take a couple minutes to look through the folders," their boss said as he reached into his pocket and took out the gold and black eagle coin that he always carried. While they read the material, he used his thumb and finger to turn it over in his hand.

He gave them ten minutes with the folders, then began speaking again, making assignments. "I'll interview Hopewell. Arriving in a plumber's truck, in case someone's watching the house. Teddy and Stinger will work the computers. Emma and Cole will go to her apartment, like they're friends dropping by. See if you can get any clues about where she was last night."

Emma glanced at Cole, thinking he probably didn't look like a friend of a millionaire's daughter. Neither did she, for that matter. She and Karen hadn't had much in common back in prep school. Karen had run with the in crowd. Emma had had a few friends, all of them outsiders.

"Stop by makeup and wardrobe and get some war paint— and something a little sexier to wear," Decorah told her. To Cole he said, "The jeans are okay but a polo shirt would look better."

They both nodded.

"Make it fast. We're working on a tight deadline. Hopewell told the kidnappers it would take him three days to get the money. Maybe he can stretch it to four, but that's pushing her safety."

Stinger and Teddy rushed off to do what they did best— get the scoop on Karen and her father.

Emma headed down the hall to make herself look a little more like a frivolous rich chick. The rich part was true. She'd never lacked for anything material growing up. But her household had never been frivolous. She'd resented her father's strict discipline, but she'd also been raised with solid values that had put her squarely on the side of people in harm's way. She'd wanted to do something important with her life, not just live off Daddy's money.

When she emerged from the prop department wearing a hot pink sweater so tight that she knew her nipples showed through the knit fabric, Cole was waiting for her. He'd exchanged the tee shirt for a baby blue polo that looked all wrong on him. But she liked the brand-new sparkling white Adidas.

Because she didn't want him to give her the once-over, she breezed past and headed straight for the Lexus pulled up at the back entrance.

He'd follow. And he'd better not make any comments.

CHAPTER TWO

Cole clenched his teeth, his gaze fixed on Emma's nicely rounded ass as he strode after her to the Lexus. She was the last person he wanted to partner with on this assignment. On any assignment, to be truthful. He had good reasons to avoid intimate contact with her.

Werewolf reasons.

He was too close to the age of bonding to be comfortable with her. Soon he'd be forced to pick a lifemate. Not because he wanted to, but because that was what his genetic heritage dictated—ever since his long-ago ancestor had dared to ask the ancient Druid gods for special powers.

He'd gotten them—for himself and the generations to follow. Dooming them to a savage life that ran parallel to ordinary men.

But they'd learned to adapt, roll with the punches, and take advantage of the modern world. In fact, Cole's current lifestyle suited him just fine. The last thing he wanted was a wife and a family, which was why he was fighting his attraction to Emma Richards, tooth and claw.

He bit back a laugh. He'd never given her any clue to his real nature, but maybe when they were alone in Karen Hopewell's apartment he could change to wolf form. That should send her running in the other direction.

Or would it?

Ever since he'd been at Decorah Security, he'd known Emma Richards was an extraordinary woman. She was trained in the martial arts. She was an expert on the gun range. And she'd taken a job as an entry-level operative with Frank Decorah, when she could have been a vice president in her dad's firm. He didn't know what she did for fun when she was off duty, but he couldn't help wondering if seeing him transform would turn her on.

Yeah sure.

He climbed behind the wheel of the luxury car, looking straight ahead. Yet he couldn't ignore her sexy pink sweater as she slid in next to him and buckled her seat belt. Had she chosen it on purpose to make him crazy? Or was she only following Decorah's directions?

The confined interior of the car was instantly filled with her tantalizing scent. Soap and woman. No perfume, thank God, because that would have overloaded his werewolf senses.

Not that he wasn't already on the edge of doing something he'd be sorry about.

He tightened his hands on the wheel and peeled out of the parking lot, headed for the Camden condo where Karen Hopewell lived.

Emma moved in her seat, drawing the sweater tighter across her breasts.

For a while neither he nor Emma spoke until he broke the silence. "So you knew her?"

"Not well. We didn't have the same interests." She swallowed hard. But I wouldn't like to be her right now. She's probably scared out of her mind."

"If she isn't drugged senseless."

Emma winced. "There's that." She cleared her throat. "You think sexual abuse is part of the scenario?"

"No way to know."

"No matter how this comes out, she's never going to be the same again,"

Cole heard the conviction in her voice. "Are you speaking from personal experience?"

"No. Thank God. I've studied cases where women have been seriously abused. I'm just putting myself in her place."

"Hopefully, they won't have her for long."

"If we can find out who's got her—and where."

They reached Karen's apartment in twenty-five minutes. It was on the second floor of a low-rise condominium complex in a Baltimore waterfront neighborhood that had undergone considerable urban renewal.

After finding a parking space around the corner, they walked back. The building's entrance was along an interior walkway, which gave them cover from the street.

Emma stood guard while Cole got out his picks and worked on the lock. They were inside so quickly that he thought Karen could have easily been taken hostage in her own home.

After making sure no one was inside, he checked escape routes. There was a sliding glass door and a balcony in the bedroom where they could exit if anyone else came nosing around

"You take the bedroom. I'll take the front of the apartment," he said to Emma, relieved that it made sense to split up.

She strode toward the back, obviously just as glad to get out of his way. Alone, he surveyed the living room. It was sleek and modern, all leather and chrome, like Karen had gone to a designer store and bought everything new. None of it looked particularly comfortable.

After glancing over his shoulder to make sure he was alone, he opened the small closet in the front hall, riffling through the coats, pulling one against his face and breathing deeply, taking in the scent of Karen Hopewell. It was young and feminine and sexy, but had nowhere near the effect on him as the fragrance of Emma Richards. However, if he picked up Karen's trail, he'd be able to follow it. That was one of his werewolf advantages—his sense of smell. It was strongest in wolf form, but even now it was far more acute than that of any human.

He had started on the kitchen, checking to see if anything was hidden in a canister of sugar, when Emma called out from the bedroom.

"Found her stash."

He put down the sugar and wiped his hands, then strode into the bedroom. A drawer was open, and Emma held up a bag of marijuana leaves.

"Want to smell it?"

He shook his head and took a quick step back. Picking up the scent of people was useful. Chemicals were another matter. Drugs played hell with a werewolf's nervous system. Even coffee and caffeinated tea were too much, which could be inconvenient in social circumstances.

"You okay."

"Of course!" he snapped, turning toward the bedside table, where he found some packets of condoms. At least she wasn't going to let her partners use the excuse that they weren't prepared. "I don't suppose you have any idea where she was snatched from?"

"I haven't spoken to her in years. And I feel weird poking through her stuff."

"Yeah."

On the dresser, he spotted a crystal bowl where Karen had thrown various odds and ends. Hard candies, a double A battery, a tube of hotel body lotion, coins, ballpoint pens. As he poked through the jumble, he found a coaster from a Baltimore club—Temptation.

"Maybe we have a clue," he said.

Emma had just put the plastic bag back under a pile of tee shirts in the drawer when the knob on the front door turned, and they both froze.

Under ordinary circumstances, Cole might have confronted the intruder, but their orders were to stay out of sight. If the kidnappers knew that Karen's father had disobeyed their instructions, they might kill the daughter.

When Emma gave him a panicked look, he took her hand and headed for the sliding glass door onto the balcony. Once they were outside, he closed the panel behind them and looked around. They could make it to the ground without too much trouble, but if they climbed down now, they might be seen. Crossing to the door at the side of the balcony, he turned the knob, and it opened.

Inside were the apartment's furnace and air conditioning system.

"In there," he whispered, entering and pulling Emma inside, before reaching behind her to shut the door.

They were plunged into instant darkness in a confined space, pressed front to front. As they both stood rigid, Cole strained his ears. His hearing was excellent, and he picked up the sound of footsteps in the apartment. A guy, or at least someone who walked heavily. Probably not a two-hundred-pound woman.

In the darkness, he could feel tension coursing through Emma. The same tension that had his guts twisting, making him feel like he was caught between heat and cold.

Heat because he wanted her with a surge of need that made his whole body tighten, and cold because they weren't playing some kid's game of hide and seek in here. If whoever was in the apartment tried the sliding glass door, they might come out here. And if they came outside, the next step was the utility closet.

In the car, he'd thought of Emma's reaction if he changed to wolf form. There wasn't room to do it in here, yet the idea had a strong appeal—at least from the tactical point of view. Whoever was in the apartment probably had a gun, but he wouldn't be expecting a wolf to leap out of hiding.

As the heavy footsteps reached the balcony, Cole slipped his arm around Emma, wanting to slide his hand up and down her back to reassure her. But that wouldn't do either

11

one of them any real good. Instead, he pulled her closer and turned her around so she wouldn't have her back to danger. Next he reached behind her with both hands to grab the inside doorknob. He braced his feet and kept his grip firm as he heard the guy coming steadily closer.

The man walked up to the door and tried to twist the knob. Cole struggled to prevent it from turning, at the same time exerting a firm pull to keep the barrier in place.

Whoever was on the other side yanked hard. Feet planted firmly on the cement, Cole kept the door from moving. When the guy finally gave up and the footsteps receded, Emma sagged against Cole, but it wasn't over quite yet. The intruder could be waiting for someone to emerge from the utility closet.

Seconds ticked by. Then minutes of silence.

"Do you think he's gone?" Emma whispered with her mouth close to Cole's ear.

"Let's hope." Cautiously Cole eased the door open and looked around, seeing no one.

When he started to step out, Emma gripped his shoulder. "Don't. It may not be safe."

"Are you worried about me?" he asked, hearing the roughness in his own voice.

"Yes,"

Suddenly it felt like she was saying yes to a whole lot more than just his flippant question. Or maybe holding her in his arms had breached the barrier he'd struggled so hard to maintain with her.

Without giving himself time to think about what he was doing, he lowered his mouth to hers. They'd known each other for a year, but it seemed like he'd been waiting an eternity for that kiss.

Had she been waiting, too? It seemed like it because the moment his lips touched hers, everything turned frantic.

In the darkness, he pulled her more tightly against himself, his hands moving up and down her back, sliding lower to cup her rounded bottom as his mouth devoured hers.

She opened for him, and he drank in the sweet taste of her. Marveled at the softness of her lips. Reveled in the twin pressure of her breasts against his chest. Shuddered at the sensation of his aching cock pressed to her middle.

She moved against him, increasing the ache.

Her hands were no less restless than his, stroking over his shoulders, his arms, reaching up to tangle in his thick hair, the intimacy of that touch increasing his arousal.

Desperate for more intimate contact, he slid his hands inward, cupping her breasts, letting their weight rest in his palms. They weren't too big. Or too small. Just right for his hands.

As he stroked his thumbs across the tightened crests, she made a moaning sound.

The first real intimacy between them, and he wanted to see her, see the passion he was certain would be shimmering in her eyes. He wanted to tear off that provocative pink sweater and her bra because they were in his way. But there was very little room in this confined space to maneuver.

Moving backwards, he pressed against the door again. But this time he wasn't holding on to the knob, and the barrier swung open, making him lose his balance.

He might have toppled onto his butt on the cement balcony, but Emma grabbed his arm, steadying him, her beautifully dilated eyes meeting his for a frantic moment before she looked away.

They were both breathing hard, and he realized that he'd been on the verge of going too far. Much too far. Which was inexcusable under the circumstances.

She let go of him abruptly, gripping the edge of the doorframe, her dilated eyes searching his face.

"What are we doing?" she asked in a strained voice.

He might have answered with a sharp comment. But that would give away too much.

Instead he straightened and cleared his throat. "I'm sorry."

"It wasn't all your fault."

Nice of her to say so. He didn't voice that comment either.

When he backed up, she followed him onto the balcony.

"There's a lot riding on this assignment. We were both on edge and worried about getting caught here" she said, making excuses for the inexcusable.

He returned his focus to the immediate situation. What if someone was still out there in the apartment?

At least they sure didn't look like a couple of private detectives.

Emma ran a shaky hand through her hair. "Who was trying to get into the utility closet, do you think?"

"Could be one of the kidnappers, making sure nobody's been in her apartment. Or one of her friends—looking for her."

"In the closet?"

"If they're worried that someone offed her and hid the body."

"What kind of lifestyle does she lead?"

"Maybe on the edge of dangerous."

Emma nodded. "I wonder how many people have her key."

He shrugged. "We'd better get out of here."

"And see what we can find out at that club. Temptation."

He moved to the sliding glass door and yanked at the handle. It was locked.

"Just great," he muttered.

All Karen wanted to do was sleep, lulled by the rocking of the narrow bed where she lay. That way, she could escape from . . .

She didn't let herself finish the thought. Instead she squeezed her eyes closed, trying to shut out the noises around her.

14

People walking past. Some of them laughing and commenting. On her. And somewhere in the background, rock music played. Proud Mary by Creedence Clearwater Revival, of all things. The bunk rolled, imitating some of the song lyrics.

A man's voice interrupted her thoughts. "I know you're awake," he said. "Stop pretending."

She slitted her eyes and saw that she was in a cage. In the middle of a lounge area. Like a lion she'd seen in Las Vegas. Only there had been barriers to keep the gamblers from getting mauled.

Looking through the bars to her left, she saw tropical greenery and a waterfall. As if this place were outside. Only she knew it wasn't. From the swaying of the bed, she thought she might be on a large ship.

She could see brightly colored parrots on stands and hear their occasional cawing.

About fifty feet from her was a structure made of bamboo. With people sitting on tall stools, drinking.

"How do you feel?"

The question brought her gaze to the man who had spoken. He was standing a few feet on the other side of the bars, staring in at her with a satisfied expression that made her stomach knot.

Dressed in gray slacks and a short-sleeved silk shirt, he was about six feet tall with medium length steel-gray hair and icy eyes.

"I said, how are you doing?"

She swallowed, trying to moisten her dry mouth enough to speak.

"Sorry about the drug. I know it's left you feeling a little rough."

He sounded pleased with himself, not sorry.

"We'll get you fixed up a little later. Hair and makeup and such. We're having a private showing tonight."

She blinked. "What?"

He let his gaze slide over her body, making her skin prickle. "You like to show off for your friends—and men who would kill to get into your pants." He laughed. "We'll give you a chance to strut your stuff tonight. Nothing too demanding. At least to start with."

She swallowed, trying to interpret what he was saying as she cautiously pushed herself to a sitting position.

"I'll have some breakfast brought around. You should eat—to keep up your strength."

"What do you mean?"

He laughed again. "More fun if you let your imagination run wild."

When he turned away, she called out. "Wait!"

Her heart raced as he kept his back to her.

When he finally turned, there was a speculative glint in his eye. "What do you want?"

"Where am I?"

"On my ship, the *Windward*."

"I want to go home."

"Of course you do, but I went to a lot of trouble to bring you here."

"Why?"

"Your father and I have a score to settle."

"What score?

"That's none of your business." He kept his gaze on her.

"Please, let me talk to him."

"That might be an interesting idea. Or perhaps something personal to you would be more effective," he said before turning away.

CHAPTER THREE

Emma walked to the railing and looked over. They were on the second floor of the condominium complex. Directly below was a cement patio bigger than the balcony.

"Not too bad a drop," she observed.

Cole eyed the hard surface. "Not under ordinary circumstances, but you don't want to twist an ankle getting down. I'll go first and help you."

She didn't want help. In fact, she didn't want him touching her again after the way they'd sent sparks flying in the closet. Unfortunately, he was right about getting injured. If she hurt herself, she wasn't going to be much good on this assignment.

That line of reasoning had a certain appeal. If she hurt herself, she could bow out and get away from Cole Marshall. Only she wasn't a coward, and she wasn't going to leave Karen Hopewell in terrible trouble. Because deep down she had a bad feeling about Karen.

She watched Cole's incredible agility as he climbed over the railing, turned, and lowered himself on strong arms to the bottom of the balcony before letting go. He was taller than she, and his feet were only dangling a yard above the ground before he landed lightly on the patio.

He looked around the area, then turned to her, holding out his arms.

17

She eased one leg over the barrier, then the other, standing so that she was facing the apartment. He had worked his hands down the upright posts, but when she tried to imitate him, the metal scraped her palms.

From the corner of her eye, she could see Cole moving behind her, and she was glad she was wearing slacks instead of a skirt.

Reaching up, he grasped her hips. "It's okay. Let go. I've got you."

She loosened her hold, letting him take her weight, then slowly lower her to the ground, the back of her body sliding against his front.

Gritting her teeth, she tried to ignore the intimacy of the contact, but that was impossible. She was sensitized to him now, and she had the conviction that if they were alone and free to follow their impulses, they would end up fucking each other's eyeballs out.

What a way to put it!

Yet that was as good a description as any.

Her feet had touched the ground, but he held on to her for another moment before dropping his hands. Gritting her teeth, she willed herself to steadiness.

"Let's get out of here," he said in a thick voice that told her he was as affected as she.

She was all for splitting. When he started around the building, she followed, then slammed into him as he stopped abruptly.

A young brunette woman was striding up the sidewalk, heading toward the back of the complex.

Cole pulled Emma out of view and they waited for the woman to pass.

When she had disappeared from sight, he stepped out and walked toward the street like they had every right to be there.

Back in the car, Emma breathed out a sigh.

"You think that woman was just a resident?" she asked.

"Odds are good, but we don't want her to remember us if anybody asks." He started the engine and headed away from the complex.

"What do we say we're doing in a nightclub at . . ." She looked at her watch. "Noon."

"Maybe we think we can get some lunch."

"Doubtful."

"I wish we could go during evening hours so we could absorb the atmosphere of the place. Only Karen doesn't have that kind of time."

"Probably like any other nightspot," Cole muttered.

"Which is what?"

He laughed. "Okay, you got me. I'm not into the club scene."

"Neither am I."

"So what do you do for fun?" he suddenly asked.

"Outdoor stuff. Jogging. Rock climbing. Jumping out of planes. Scuba diving."

"I haven't tried the jumping part."

"But the rest?" she asked, thinking that they'd hardly talked about their private lives.

"You thought I stayed home and watched football?"

She laughed. "I guess not."

"I have some property on the Eastern Shore. Near Easton. I got it cheap because it was pretty run-down. I spend the weekends there fixing the place up."

"Nice to be handy."

"Yeah," he answered, his tone telling her that the personal conversation was making him edgy.

They drove in silence the rest of the way to Temptation—which had a black slab front with no windows and no hint of what was inside except for the name of the club in silver letters across the door. Which probably meant that the place didn't need to advertise.

After circling the block, they drove up the alley, noting the exits before they parked.

19

"We're friends of Karen's," Cole said before they got out. "We're worried about her because we were supposed to get together today. And she's talked about this place, so we thought we'd see if anyone knows where she is."

"Sounds like a plan."

"Act casual."

As they walked toward the door, he reached for her hand. She might have jerked away, but she told herself the posture was part of their cover.

Still, his calloused fingers against her softer ones sent tingling sensations all the way up her arm.

"You do the talking," she said.

"Okay."

Inside, it took a moment for their eyes to adjust to the dim light.

It turned out that there were a few customers at the bar, even this early in the day. Across the room were some tables and low-backed chairs. Above a large dance floor metallic streamers dangled. Probably at night they glittered. At noon, they just looked limp.

"Help you?" the bartender asked. He was a tall guy with a thick mane of dark hair who probably doubled as a bouncer. The sleeves of his white button-down shirt were rolled up to the elbows.

Cole gave the story about Karen that they'd agreed on.

"I saw her here last night," the bartender said.

"Did she leave with anyone?"

"I wasn't paying attention."

A bleached blond waitress wearing a low cut black top, black miniskirt and fishnet stockings joined the conversation. "She wasn't *with* anyone, but when she left, a guy hurried right out after her."

"Good to know," Cole said. "You think she'll be back tonight?"

"Might be," the bartender said.

"Could you let her know Jimmy and Pam are looking for her," he asked.

When the bartender looked doubtful, Cole handed him a twenty, which he slipped into his pocket.

There was nothing more they could do. Bombarding the staff with questions was going to look out of character for the casual friends they were supposed to be.

"Jimmy and Pam," Emma said in a low voice as they stood on the sidewalk. "That's not going to get us anything for your twenty bucks."

"You think he's going to call?" Cole shot back. "She's not coming back here because she's not free to, but tipping the bartender for information reinforces our cover."

"Okay," she murmured, acknowledging his logic.

As they walked toward the car, a flicker of movement caught her eye, and she looked around to see a big guy who could have been a Mr. Universe contender heading purposefully toward them. He was over six feet tall wearing jeans and a tee shirt that showed off his bulging muscles. From the heavy way he walked, he could be the guy who'd checked out the apartment.

Cole had seen him too. He glanced quickly back toward the club. "Get back inside. I'll lead him away."

She didn't like that option, but the look on Cole's face told her that an argument would simply waste precious time.

And she understood the wisdom of the ploy, especially if they were supposed to be Karen's friends and not trained security operatives. Civilians would flee—not stand and fight.

Teeth gritted, she reversed directions, ducking in the side door of the club, while Cole took off in the other direction.

Mr. Universe hesitated. Probably he thought the woman was a better target, but he wasn't going to get her without alerting the staff.

She found herself in a service hallway.

"Hey!" a guy in a waiter's uniform exclaimed. "If you're looking for the little girls' room, it's not back here."

"Please let me stay for a minute. Some guy came after me in the parking lot."

He grunted. "Like that blond last night. Karen Hopewell."

"You saw what happened to her?"

"Yeah. I was outside taking a smoke break."

"Did you call the police?"

He gave her a defiant look. "I stay away from the cops."

She sighed, understanding his motivation. It was a good bet that he had a record, and he didn't want to get involved and maybe lose his job.

"Can you tell me about it?"

"They shoved her into a car."

"More than one man?"

"Yeah."

"What did they look like?"

"It was dark. I didn't see much. Two big guys with broad shoulders. One of them was bald. I saw light gleaming off his dome."

"But you're sure it was Karen Hopewell?"

"She stands out. Lots of guys on the dance floor were looking at her."

"Uh huh."

"You told Ed you're a friend of hers."

"Right."

He gave her a long look. "You don't look like someone she'd run with."

"Because?"

"You don't wear enough makeup."

"I do at night," she answered absently, thinking that she needed to share what she'd just learned with Cole.

Where was he? And was it safe to go out now?

Cautiously she opened the door a crack and looked out. Although there was no sign of Cole, she spotted something that made the hairs on the back of her neck prickle.

A dozen yards away, Mr. Universe was down on the pavement, and a big dog—a German shepherd it looked like—

was on top of him, growling and snapping at the hand the guy had raised in a defensive move.

Or maybe it wasn't a dog. Maybe it was a wolf.

A wolf in the middle of Baltimore? Unlikely.

The man was trying to protect his face and getting his fingers nipped. Emma had the impression that the animal could kill him if it wanted, but it was acting with restraint. Which was strange.

Maybe he saw the door open, because he looked up, and for a moment their eyes met.

That split second was enough of a distraction for the big guy to leap up and take off in the other direction like the devil was after him.

The wolf stared at Emma for heartbeats, looking like he wanted to run toward her. Instead he turned and raced off, following the man.

When he disappeared around the corner, Emma sagged against the doorframe, trying to figure out what she'd just seen.

Before she'd gone into the club, Cole had run in the other direction, and the bodybuilder had followed him. The next thing she'd seen was a big dog or a wolf attacking the man.

She was still standing beside the kitchen door when Cole appeared around the corner, running toward her, looking like he'd taken off his clothes and put them back on in a hurry. He was tugging at the hem of his shirt as he drew close to her.

"Are you all right?" she asked breathlessly.

"Fine."

"Where were you?"

"Trying to lead him away from you."

She nodded.

"Did he double back when he couldn't catch me?"

"Yes," she answered in a shaky voice. "And a big dog was mauling him—over there," she pointed to the spot where the dog had cornered the guy.

23

"Too bad for him. Did you find out anything when you went back inside?"

"Yes."

"We'd better get out of here before he comes back. You can tell me in the car."

She nodded, fighting the feeling that he was trying to direct her attention away from the guy and the dog.

Just then her cell phone rang, and she fished it out of her pocket.

It was Frank Decorah. "Get back to the office ASAP. There's been a new development," the chief said.

CHAPTER FOUR

On the way to Beltsville, Cole listened as Emma told him what she'd learned from the waiter, but his mind was churning. In the club, he'd definitely detected Karen Hopewell's scent among the rich mixture of odors. Then in the alley, he'd figured the wolf was his best chance for getting the drop on the guy who was after them, and he'd acted instinctively without thinking about Emma—or anybody else—seeing him.

When he'd told her his story, she'd looked at him strangely, like she wasn't sure if he was telling the truth about what had happened.

But he wasn't about to alter his version of events. Not until he was forced to. He was starting to wonder if that might happen sooner than he wanted.

They made it to the office in a half hour, and he was glad to get out of the confines of the car.

The team was waiting in the conference room.

Granada and Henderson were looking pretty pleased with themselves, but they let Emma tell about what she and Cole had learned—leaving out the unprofessional behavior in the utility closet, of course.

When she was done, Decorah turned to Stinger. "Give them what you've got."

"Computer traffic from the *Windward*."

"Which is?" Cole asked.

"A yacht motoring off the coast of Florida. Well, it's outside U.S. waters. I say yacht for convenience. It's really a decommissioned cruise ship, owned by a guy named Bruno Del Conte. His mother was German and his father was Italian. They met when Hitler and Mussolini were partnering it up during World War II. The mom did some spying for the Axis. The dad enriched himself with property confiscated from Italian Jews."

"Nice pair."

"The son had all the rich kid advantages. Private school in Milan. An estate on Lake Como where he could bring his college friends. And he kept up the family tradition of opportunism. His latest enterprise is a very upscale pleasure palace—for men and women who want to indulge their sexual fantasies."

Cole whistled through his teeth. "Wait a minute. You're saying some guy owns a whole cruise ship?"

"All fifty thousand tons. He's rich enough to own anything he wants. Well, maybe not the Great Wall of China. But he thinks on a scale most people can't imagine, and he's got a beef with Karen Hopewell's father. Looks like they were both going after a big block of shares in the same hotel chain. Hopewell made an end run around Del Conte and picked up the stock for less than it was worth."

"Any idea how?" Emma asked.

Frank sighed. "Hopewell and I go way back. But I know he's not above using methods the SEC might not approve of. That was five years ago, and Del Conte has been mad about it ever since."

"So shanghaiing the daughter and asking for money would be a way to get back at Hopewell," Cole mused.

"That's a good bet."

"Why would he wait so long?"

"Maybe he wanted Hopewell to think he was in the clear before striking."

"But how do we know he's got her?" Emma pressed.

"We don't—not for absolute sure. But it's a ninety-seven percent probability," Stinger put in.

"Based on what?" Emma asked.

"A lot of factors," Teddy answered. "Del Conte's proclivity for holding a grudge until he figures out a creative way to get even. Like he once let a business rival buy a resort in the Swiss Alps, then burned the place down the day after the guy took possession."

"There's proof of that?"

"Not something you could take to court, although the signs all point to Del Conte. But back to the current situation. Yesterday, a helicopter flight landed on the *Windward*, and there's no record of the cargo or passengers. Plus heightened security. Something special is going on over there."

"Is that enough to bet Karen Hopewell's life on?"

"Not by itself. But we also picked up an e-mail message from one of the guards on board to his pregnant wife back in Miami. After that we went back and scanned his other communications with her. He needed a job, so he signed up for ship security. Apparently he didn't know what he was getting into. He hates the place and wants to get another job, but he's trapped because they need the money with the baby coming. In the current e-mail he's explaining why he can't come home this weekend, like he said he would. All leave was canceled because they have a special guest, and the whole place is on alert."

"That sounds like it could be Karen," Cole mused.

"We have a schematic of the ship. There's a section of the passenger area that's off-limits to everyone except the crew and trusted guests. That might be where they're holding her. I'm hoping you can get in there and find out. Then spring her."

Emma shifted in her seat. "But we're building this case on supposition. What if we're wrong? Did you learn anything from your interview with Hopewell?"

"Only that he's worried sick, and he blames himself for putting his daughter at risk."

"Does he think it could be Del Conte?"

"He thinks it's a possibility."

"But there aren't any hard facts," Cole muttered.

"We're going to hedge our bets," their boss said, reaching for his eagle coin again and starting to flip it in his hand. "You and Emma are going on board as paying guests. We'll have a team tailing the *Windward* in case you find Karen. And if she's not on the ship, we'll keep searching for clues in Baltimore and on the Web. Maybe we can locate that goon who went after you in Baltimore and make him talk."

"Probably he's one of the guys who pushed her into that car," Cole said. He watched Emma swallow.

"What do guests do on the *Windward*?" she asked.

"Nothing but fun. For them."

"Oh right."

"Which is?"

"Sexual fantasy scenarios. S and M relationships. If you can think of it, he can arrange it. He's got a whole group of employees who play the role of slaves. Or masters if that's what the guest wants."

She grimaced, and Cole thought she was probably imagining the girl she'd known forced into that role. Too bad knowing Karen made the assignment more personal.

"We're wasting time. We've got to bring you up to speed on everything we know about Del Conte," Decorah said. "But one thing I want to say to the group before we break off. There are women who come to the ship from foreign countries who serve as hostesses. Some of them disappear, and we have to assume that either they were forced into a sex game that got them killed—or they were sold into slavery. Not the pretend slaves on the ship."

28

Emma gasped, a look of horror blooming on her face. "Killed? How?"

"Some of the guests come to the *Windward* because they like to engage in questionable activities, away from the prying eyes of the authorities. The *Windward* is closer than some of the Asian countries where they can indulge their tastes. If one of them got carried away, he could kill his partner. Or maybe there are special girls designated for death scenarios."

Emma's face contorted. "That's sick."

"So is the human trafficking angle. God knows what happens to *those* women."

She shuddered, and Cole could see that the information was churning in her mind. Suddenly the idea of sending her into that nest of vipers made his stomach knot."

"Leave Emma out of it," he heard himself say.

Decorah swung toward him, a surprised look on his face.

"It's too dangerous for her. I can handle it on my own."

Decorah's expression turned hard. "You aren't superman. You need a backup."

Emma fixed her gaze on Cole. "I don't want *you* taking this on alone."

He had already said that he didn't want her going in at all. Short of quitting, he knew he was stuck with an assignment he hated. And if he quit, he was afraid from Emma's reaction that she would take the risk anyway.

Feeling trapped, he asked, "When are we leaving?"

CHAPTER FIVE

Karen was sitting hunched over, trying to make herself as small as possible when two burly men stepped up to the door of the cage.

When one of them punched an electronic keypad, she shrank back.

The guy stood looking at her for a long moment that made her stomach tighten into a painful knot. She wanted to plead with him, but she knew it would do no good.

"Come on," he growled.

When she didn't step forward, he strode into the cell and grabbed her arm. I said, "Come on."

"Where?"

"You'll find out."

Never in a million lifetimes would she have thought she could end up in this situation. She'd had a wonderful life. Was the operative word *had*?

Were they going to kill her? Rape her? Or what? She struggled not to cry as they marched her out of the cell, past the potted greenery, down a set of stairs, along a corridor, and into a suite of rooms.

Everything was so totally different from her cell that she blinked as she tried to decide if it was real or if her mind had stopped coping with reality.

It looked like she was in the mauve and silver waiting room of an upscale beauty salon with comfortable couches and glass-topped coffee tables with current women's magazines. Well, come to think of it, not quite like any salon she'd been in. Also on the tables were bondage magazines, judging from the covers. And big glossy books with pictures of naked men. As well as illustrated guides to tattooing and body piercing.

Along the far wall were shelves of high end hair and beauty products mixed with shelves of what looked like sex toys.

No other patrons were in the waiting room, but two women in black uniforms stood near the wall. One was a tall, willowy blond whose name tag identified her as Allison. The other was a stunningly beautiful, petite Asian woman. Her long dark hair was artfully streaked and her nails were a bright crimson. She wore a name tag that said she was Anna.

She seemed to be the one in charge. Raising her chin, she addressed the guards. "Wait outside."

"Mr. Del Conte's orders . . ."

"I must have complete access to our guest."

The man glared down at the tiny woman. "The master will hear about this."

She raised her chin. "There's only one exit to this salon. Wait at the door."

There was a moment when Karen wasn't sure who would win out, the big man or the petite woman. Finally the man shrugged. When he and his companion exited the room, the two attendants exchanged glances.

"Which of us is going to stay with her?" Allison asked.

Anna shrugged. "It's all the same to me."

"Then you do it. I want to take off my polish and redo my nails."

"Fine."

The blond stepped into another room, and the Asian woman held out her arm. "Come with me."

31

Karen's mind was spinning. The guard had said, "Mr. Del Conte." A couple of times, she'd been in the office and heard her father mention that name with either a snarl or a sneer in his voice. He was a business rival, she thought. Someone Daddy detested.

Was he the man who had spoken to her earlier? When she was in that cage. She shuddered.

Anna interrupted her thoughts.

"The master wants you to look your best."

"The . . . the master? That's Mr. Del Conte?"

"Yes," Anna answered.

"What does he want from me?

"He doesn't confide in me. I just manage the salon. And you are not here to ask me questions," the woman said sternly.

"We're on a ship, right?"

"Yes."

Before she could get any more information, Anna said, "Come. We have limited time, and I will be punished if I do not complete my assignment. "

Karen glanced back toward the door. The two men were out there. She might knock out this woman, but then what? Allison would probably come running.

Maybe Anna saw the expression on Karen's face because she fixed her with a steely look. "No," she mouthed.

Karen answered with a small nod. It looked like her only option was to cooperate for now—and hope she could escape later.

Anna led her down a short hall to a large, marble bathroom with a shower.

"I'm sure you'd like to clean up," she said.

"Yes. Thank you."

"You will have ten minutes to shower and wash your hair."

Anna leaned into the shower and turned on the water, then stepped toward the door.

"Get undressed. Throw your ruined clothes in the trash. Then take your shower. When the timer rings, get out and dry yourself. I'll be waiting for you outside."

Karen quickly took off her wrinkled clothing and stuffed it in the trash receptacle, feeling self-conscious. Someone could be watching her on a hidden camera, but there was nothing she could do about that. Anxious to get clean, she stepped into the shower.

It was wonderful to stand under the hot spray. As the water poured out of the shower head, she raised her face and closed her eyes, grateful to be alone for a few minutes.

Or was she?

A low grating voice made her jump. "No matter what you hear, don't turn around. Keep on with what you're doing. Some of us are preparing to escape. Maybe we can help you."

Karen's throat clogged. She wanted to turn, but she obeyed directions.

In a moment, the door closed, and she knew she was alone again.

Who had spoken? It had been a woman. Most likely Anna or Allison, but she couldn't be sure which because the voice had been disguised.

As she washed, she tried to figure it out, but she simply couldn't.

At least the hot water helped ease some of her tension, and when she opened a bottle of shampoo, grapefruit scent wafted toward her.

She longed to stay in here for hours, washing off the fear and humiliation of the past few hours, but she had no doubt that she must conform to the time constraint.

Quickly she washed her hair and applied cream rinse. She was almost finished when the timer rang. With a shudder, she stepped out, turned off the water, then dried herself with a fluffy towel, tucking it around her body as Anna came back.

"Come on. This way."

Taking a chance, Karen asked, "Did you speak to me in the shower?"

"Certainly not!" She pointed to another doorway, and Karen saw a treatment room beyond. In it was a salon chair and a padded table.

"We'll start getting you ready."

"You said you had some clothes for me?"

"Later. Lie down on the table."

"For what?"

"The master wants your pubic hair shaved."

Karen sucked in a sharp breath. The look might be popular, but she'd never liked it. "Why?"

"Lie down. Unless you want me to call the guards back to help hold you still."

"No," she whispered as she climbed onto the padded table and closed her eyes.

"Then later we'll make you look pretty for the people in the Tropical Lounge. I have a butterfly ornament you'll love."

In a room not far away, a group of men sat in comfortable easy chairs facing a large flat-screen television. They ranged in age from their early forties well into their seventies. All had the satisfied aspect of men who were used to getting what they wanted—as long as they were willing to pay for it. No questions asked.

One of them took a drag on a fat Havana cigar and blew out smoke.

"She's a real looker. That red hair is stunning. An unusual color. And it's real, too." He laughed.

"Lovely."

"Where did you get her?"

"Her father did me a disservice."

The questioner laughed.

"I loved the way her breasts looked in the shower when she raised her hands to wash her hair."

"She seems so vulnerable. And frightened."

"She'll feel more vulnerable with her pussy shaved."

"Who gets to fuck her first?"

Bruno Del Conte cut through the chatter, his voice brusque. "Nobody. Unless I decide on it. I have some other activities in mind for her."

"The whipping post?"

"Perhaps."

A gray-haired man licked his lips before speaking. "I'd like to see her tied down while two slaves arouse her."

"Maybe she can't respond with an audience."

"With drugs, she will."

"Okay. Yeah. Then untie one of her hands and make her masturbate in front of us."

"Make the two slaves a man and a woman. Could we have that hot little Asian hairdresser as part of the scene?"

"While the new girl sucks the guy's cock."

"No, that's going too fast. More fun to draw out her education in her new life."

"Do you think she likes to stick her finger inside herself when she makes herself come?"

"Or touch her breasts? Got to untie two hands for all of that."

"One of the slaves can play with her breasts while she does the cunt part."

"A light whip across her nipples would be more interesting."

"I'd like to see her in the mirror room, where she can look at herself from all angles while slaves oil her body—all over."

Others made their own suggestions, revealing their sexual tastes.

A fifty-year-old man stood up abruptly, his face flushed, his breathing uneven and his cock pushing out the front of his slacks. "I'm going down to the fantasy floor. I want to look over the slave girls and pick out two. Have a group of them ready when I arrive."

"Any other specifications?" Del Conte asked.

"They have a record of what I like."

Del Conte watched him leave, his expression thoughtful. He'd started off on the assumption that he might sell Karen back to her father after putting her through some unpleasant experiences that she would never forget. Now it looked like it would be more fun to keep her on the ship, but he was certainly going to leave his options open.

He'd be giving up five million dollars in favor of fees from guests, but money wasn't the real issue. It was revenge. Maybe the best way to make Hopewell suffer was to send him a series of videos that would make his hair stand on end.

The mention of hair gave him an idea. Picking up the phone, he placed a call to the beauty salon.

Anna picked up on the first ring.

"I want a lock of her hair delivered to my office. Put it in a plastic bag, along with some of her pubic hair."

"Yes, sir."

"We're taking a plane to Fort Lauderdale right now," Frank Decorah told Emma and Cole. I'll come along to brief you."

Cole winced. That was certainly getting things rolling at lightning speed, but he understood the urgency. Given the description he'd just heard, there was no telling what had already happened to Karen Hopewell on that damn ship.

The boss drove them to a small airport between Baltimore and Washington where an executive jet was waiting.

Cole was glad the boss was going with them because he still had a lot of questions. Which he hoped Decorah was going to answer.

The passenger cabin was laid out like a lounge, with comfortable seating around the bulkhead, facing inward. There was also a service area stocked with sandwiches, since they had skipped lunch.

Cole wasn't very hungry, but he took apart a couple of rare roast beef sandwiches and ate the meat.

"What are you doing?" Emma asked.

"Low carb diet."

"You?"

He shrugged and picked up one of the briefing folders that Decorah had put on the table in the center of the cabin.

It had the schematic of the ship, speculation about the specific activities in the entertainment areas, and a lot of information on Del Conte.

He was fifty-five and kept himself in excellent shape with regular workouts in his ship's extensive gym. He'd gotten a degree in finance from the London School of Economics and used his inheritance from his father as a springboard to even greater wealth—often by criminal or at least questionable means. His floating resort was probably an outgrowth of his own sexual interests. And his need for control. Having a whole ship full of people who did his bidding reinforced his image of himself as a man of power.

He had never been married and never had a girlfriend who was with him for more than a few years.

Cole wondered he'd paid them off with a nice parting gift or if they'd ended up dead. It didn't seem likely that any of them would dare to leave the guy—unless they went into hiding. But he didn't voice that thought to Emma. She was looking unsettled enough as she read the report.

"When the ship is at sea, there are two ways for guests to arrive," Frank said, interrupting Cole's thoughts. "Chopper and hovercraft. No one is authorized to come in by air at the moment, which is another indication that something unusual is going on there."

Emma nodded.

"Since I was pretty sure you'd be going to the *Windward*, I had a suitable wardrobe packed for both of you. You'll be leaving for the hovercraft shortly after we land, so you should change into resort clothes now."

Cole glanced at Emma. She looked tense but resigned.

Frank gave her the kind of critical look that Cole knew she detested. When he'd first joined Decorah Security, he had dug into her background. He knew her father had drummed old-fashioned values and morality into his offspring. He had also demanded more from his children than they could possible give. Her brother had responded by becoming a drug addict. Emma had gone the other way. She pushed herself to the max but bristled when anyone else pushed her too hard.

He also knew she had never had a serious relationship that had lasted more than a year, which suggested that she had a commitment problem.

He couldn't argue with that. He had the same problem, only for a different reason. He liked his life fine the way it was, and the thought of settling down made his skin prickle.

"Try to act like you're anticipating a good time," Frank advised, speaking to both of them.

"Right," she clipped out, standing up and reaching for the carry bag that the director indicated. She took it to the head in the back and returned a few minutes later wearing white shorts that barely covered her ass and a halter top.

"I love being turned into a sex object," she muttered as she sat back in her seat.

Cole understood her point, but he couldn't help admiring the way the clothing set off her high breasts and long legs.

He took his own bag to the back and found lightweight tan slacks to go with his baby blue polo shirt. A lot more comfortable than Emma's outfit.

Emma's eyes went from Cole to Frank and back again. "What—exactly—is our cover?" she asked.

"We're keeping it as simple as possible. Cole's a wealthy playboy named Cole Mason who lives off the money he inherited from his rich parents. You have a little business that does custom detailing for luxury cars, mostly because you like to add weird stuff to your own vehicles."

"Super."

38

He looked at Emma. "You're his current girlfriend. Like Del Conte, he hasn't formed any attachments that last more than a few years."

"He'll check my background," Cole muttered.

"Granada and Henderson have taken care of that. You've got a history he can look up on the Web. Starting with your getting kicked out of half a dozen private colleges."

Cole winced.

"Use the rest of the time to read about yourself." He turned to Emma. "You too. Briefly, you're Emma Ray. Until a couple of months ago, you were a waitress in a cocktail bar in Denver. Cole came in and swept you off your feet. Or, at least, he offered you a lifestyle you couldn't afford on your own. Like many women down through the ages, you saw the advantages of being the mistress of a wealthy man."

"And what's supposed to happen to me when he gets tired of the mistress?" Emma snapped.

"Maybe you can make it turn out like that movie—Pretty Woman."

She snorted.

Cole kept his gaze focused on the briefing book, but he saw Emma clutch the edge of the folder. She hadn't been assigned a very appealing role, but then neither had he.

They both concentrated on their own background material for the rest of the trip to Florida, except when Frank took Cole into the back of the plane for a short private conference.

"You know I'm hoping your special talents will bring Karen home," he said.

"I figured. If I can pick up her scent, I can find her. But getting her out of there isn't going to be so easy."

"I hate that old cliché—I'm counting on you. But it's true."

"You're not expecting me to turn into a wolf in the middle of one of Del Conte's playrooms, are you?"

"Probably not. But maybe the wolf will come in handy."

Cole nodded. He had a relationship with Frank that went deep. The Decorah chief had saved his life, then practically adopted him. Before Cole met Frank, he'd been content with his high school education. Frank had paid for college and graduate school, and Cole had discovered he liked using his brains as well as his brawn.

He'd learned a hell of a lot from Frank, and not just about the security business, although the man's insights were the cornerstone of his own expertise. And he was always going to be grateful—for all of it.

As they came back, Emma gave them a long look. When neither one of them enlightened her about the private conversation, she went back to her briefing book, but he knew she was bristling at being excluded.

As far as he was concerned, the flight was over much too quickly.

They landed at a small airfield outside Fort Lauderdale, where a rental car was waiting. A supercharged Infinity sports model, as per Cole's supposed rich guy—car freak—status.

Before they left for the marina where Del Conte's hovercraft would pick them up, Decorah had a few more things to say.

"There's a transmitter in Emma's purse. In her lipstick. You won't be able to send a message because that would give you away. But when you're ready to leave, twist the bottom of the tube and it will send a signal to the boat we'll have waiting to pick you and Karen Hopewell up."

"What if they don't get there in time?"

"You might have to swim away from the ship."

"Oh great," Emma muttered.

"You can swim, can't you?" Frank Decorah snapped, and it was obvious that he was feeling the strain of the assignment.

"You know I'm a strong swimmer, but what if one of us is injured?"

"The other two will have to help get him or her to the boat."

"You're sure Karen Hopewell is comfortable in the water?" Cole asked.

"Her father says she can swim."

They left the airport alone in the rental car, heading for the *Windward* private dock.

As he drove, Cole glanced over at Emma. "Did you like Karen?"

"Not a lot. I thought she was spoiled, but I wouldn't wish this on anyone." She paused, then went on, "Maybe she's grown up since I knew her."

"Yeah." He cleared his throat. 'We should discuss our relationship," he said in a tight voice.

When she jumped, he realized she thought he was talking about the fallout from the kiss in the utility closet. Which both of them wished had never happened.

"I mean—the relationship of the characters we're playing. Cole Mason and Emma Ray."

"Oh, right."

He clenched his hands on the wheel, wishing they could skip this discussion but knowing he had to make things clear. "If the ship is set up for people who want to indulge their fantasies, that could be dangerous for you. I mean, you're very attractive, and some other guy might want to . . ." He stopped and started again. "We'd better make it that I'm very possessive of you. That way, if Del Conte or anybody else wants to . . ." He stopped again and cleared his throat, "use you for anything . . . weird, I have a reason to object."

Emma had been staring straight ahead. When she flicked her gaze to Cole, she was shocked by the expression on his face—something between determined and grossed out. Until then, she hadn't realized how much he hated this assignment. But it was more than that. She also saw worry etched on his features, and it wasn't for himself. He cared about her welfare, and that astonished her. She'd always

41

thought of him as hard-bitten and self-contained. Apparently that was what he'd *wanted* her to see.

She had the sudden conviction that he'd been attracted to her all along—but he'd been fighting it. Why? Because he didn't think an office romance was appropriate?

She longed to lay her hand over his and tell him everything was going to work out all right, but she couldn't get the words past her suddenly tight throat.

Decorah was putting them into a very dangerous situation.

Cole could have bailed out. Or she could. But here they were together. Because they were both committed to rescuing a girl who'd gotten caught in the middle of something bad—through no fault of her own. It didn't matter that she had known Karen, and Cole hadn't. They'd both do their best to rescue her.

But what had Decorah said to Cole that he wanted to keep between the two of them? She'd like to ask, but she was afraid she wasn't going to get an answer. And if she did ask, it was only going to increase the tension between them.

Cole broke into her thoughts.

"Another thing—we have assume that there are surveillance cameras all over the ship. Maybe even in our bedroom. Or at the very least that the room will be bugged."

She dragged in a sharp breath. "Cameras in our bedroom? Isn't that an invasion of privacy?"

He answered with a mirthless laugh. "Of course it is, but you've got to wrap your mind around Del Conte's thinking. If some of his guests will pay to see what other guests are doing in private, why not take advantage of that? I mean, suppose you met someone in the bar and you wondered what he liked to do that he didn't want to talk about. You could watch him."

"If that's the way your mind works."

"Remember, this is a place where all the rules of civilized society are out the window. Which is a good reason to have the security staff keeping tabs on everyone."

"Lord, I didn't think about all of that." She turned toward him. "If we're being watched, how do we communicate with each other?"

"Do you know Morse code?"

"No."

"Too bad."

"You do?"

"Yeah. It can come in handy. Like to tap dots and dashes on a partner's hand."

She grimaced. Too bad nobody had ever suggested she might need that communications method one day."

Cole's voice turned reassuring. "It's okay. We'll have to decide how to talk in private after we get there."

She wished they could settle the problem now, but she knew that he was right. It was going to depend on the situation.

Her throat was suddenly dry, but she managed to ask. "And how much are we going to have to participate in the fun and games?"

"Do I know?"

"I guess not."

He waited a beat before saying, "Obviously, I'm the dominant member in our relationship."

"Huh?"

"I'm talking about the way we treat each other in our roles. I'm the one with the money and power. That means you do what you think will please me."

"Now wait a minute."

"I'm still talking about our cover story. How we treat each other on the ship in public—and in private."

She gave him a hard look. "And suppose *you've* come here with me because you like to play the submissive sometimes. And this is a place you feel comfortable letting your hair

43

down, where you buddies won't cotton to your secret desires."

His response was adamant. "Out of the question. I am not going to put myself in that position."

"You're young and fit. Being submissive might make you seem less threatening to Del Conte."

He considered that. "You could be right, but I'm sure I wouldn't be a very convincing bottom."

"What the hell is a bottom?"

"A submissive."

"You've studied this stuff."

"I've studied a lot of stuff."

"And you think I'll be a convincing—bottom?"

"Let's hope so."

She gave him a long look. "Do you have some reason to think I can play that role?"

"Because of your father?"

"What?" She heard the shock ring in her voice. "What about my father?" she managed to add. "You don't think he and I ever . . ."

"No. It wouldn't have fit into his moral code. But he's a very dominating man."

"How the hell do you know anything about him?"

He signed. "I wouldn't work with someone if I didn't have a handle on their background."

"Pull over," she ordered.

"What?"

"I said pull over."

He eased to the shoulder of the road, set the emergency brake, and turned to her. "What—are you backing out."

"No," she said between gritted teeth. "But I want you to know that I don't appreciate your digging into my private life."

"Noted."

"Too bad I didn't check you out, too. What is it that you're hiding about yourself?"

"Nothing!"

"That's a lie." She dragged in a breath and let it out before asking. "And what did Frank Decorah say to you that he didn't want me to hear."

He waited a beat before answering. "That he was counting on my expertise to get Karen out."

"What expertise do you have that I don't?"

He kept his gaze steady. "An over-developed sense of smell."

"Jesus. If I even believe that—how is it going to help."

"I picked up her scent in her apartment. And in Temptation. I'll know if she's on the boat. And where to find her."

She glared at him, wondering if he was spinning her a line.

When he covered her hand with his, she jumped.

"This is a bad time to get into an argument," he said in a low voice.

She nodded.

His hand tightened on hers. "We're both tense. Under a lot of pressure. Feeling like we don't have enough preparation. At least, that's true for me."

"Agreed."

"We need to settle down. Be comfortable with each other. Our lives could depend on it."

"I know."

He swallowed hard. "You're right. There's stuff in my background that I don't talk about. I'm from a very dysfunctional family. And when we get back to Maryland, I'll tell you about it."

"You will?" she asked, genuinely shocked.

"Yeah."

"Why not now?"

"Because it would be a distraction, and we have to focus on rescuing Karen Hopewell."

"Okay," she whispered.

"So are we as ready as we're going to be."

"Yes."

He released the brake, and started off again.

When she stole a glance at his face, it was set in a grim line. What the hell was his background, anyway? Too bad she hadn't done the kind of prying that he'd indulged in. Or was it something so well hidden that she wouldn't have found it anyway.

Leaning back she closed her eyes, breathing deeply, struggling for calm—and for the character she was playing.

Still, when she felt the car slow, her stomach tightened.

Opening her eyes, she saw a sign that said "*Windward* Dock. Authorized persons only."

As Cole pulled into a parking space, his cell phone rang. He glanced at Emma, then clicked it on.

"Glad I caught you," Frank Decorah said, speaking loud enough for both of them to hear. "There's been a development. A lock of Karen's hair was just delivered to her father, along with some of her pubic hair."

Emma dragged in a breath. "With a note?" I assume.

"No. Only the hair."

"You're sure it's hers?" Cole asked.

"As you saw in the photo, it's a very unusual shade."

"Better than chopping off her ear," Cole said, referring to the J. Paul Getty grandson who'd been kidnapped years ago—and finally returned to his family after they paid a sizable ransom.

"Was the pubic hair pulled out or shaved?" Emma asked.

"Shaved."

"Thanks for the information," Cole said before clicking off.

"They shaved her pubic hair," Emma murmured. "That's pretty nasty. I mean if it was against her will."

"Another indication of what we're getting into."

"We've got to assume he did it so he can display her."

Emma nodded, struggling to stay objective. "It sounds like I need to check out the beauty salon when we get on board.

There's some chance that she's not on the *Windward*, but maybe I can confirm it in the beauty shop."

"Yeah." Cole's voice had turned thoughtful as he looked at the phone he was still holding, then pressed some buttons, erasing the record of the call. "They'd take this away from me on the ship, and I don't want them checking my contact list. Instead of slipping the phone back into his pocket, he shoved it into the crevice between the console and the driver's seat, where it slipped down out of sight.

"Will they search for it?" Emma asked.

"If they do, they'll have a devil of a time finding it." He looked at Emma. "Get rid of yours, too." She sent her phone to meet his, then swallowed hard and opened the passenger door.

She swallowed hard and opened the passenger door.

Before they could take the luggage out of the trunk, a muscular man in his thirties wearing a dark suit and captain's type hat came rushing over. His name tag identified him as Greg.

"Mr. Mason? Ms. Ray?"

"Yes."

"Welcome to the *Windward*. Let me get your luggage."

Cole opened the trunk, and the man picked up both their bags.

"You're traveling light," he said.

"I was hoping to buy some new outfits on board," Emma murmured. "There's a women's shop—right?"

"Yes. Several. You can buy anything from a formal gown to a peasant outfit. There's also a lingerie boutique. And if you want to buy costumes for special occasions, we have them, too."

"Costumes?" Emma asked.

"If you like a role you've played on the ship and want to duplicate it at home. And you can buy the toys to go along with it."

He laughed. "Of course, you may want those shipped."

47

"How come?"

"They might be embarrassing at airport security."

"Oh—right," she managed, then glanced at Cole. "You're not going to mind if I do some shopping are you, sweetie?"

"Just don't get too carried away, darling," he answered.

They followed Greg to the hovercraft waiting at the dock. It looked large enough to hold a hundred passengers if the seating had been arranged in rows, but they appeared to be the only ones on board besides Greg, a couple of other similarly dressed attendants, and the working crew dressed in blue and white striped shirts and dark pants.

The seats were comfortable sofas and plush armchairs bolted to the deck, grouped around low coffee tables. The backs of each sofa and chair were high, giving a feeling of privacy. Each seating arrangement had a flat-screen television set on a console, with a privacy screen in back.

Emma let Cole lead her to a grouping in the middle of the cabin. As she pondered where to sit, he gently pulled her onto the couch beside him.

"All set?"

"Yes," Cole answered.

Greg gave a signal, and the powerful engines revved up. As the hovercraft headed out to sea, the steward said, "It's about an hour ride. How can I make you comfortable? Champagne? Hors d'oeuvres?" He picked up the remote that was attached by a retractable cord to the coffee table. "We have a variety of entertainment. Just press the power button, and then scroll through the channels."

"Thank you. Nothing to eat or drink. We just had lunch." He kept his gaze fixed on the steward. "I was hoping we could come in by chopper. That would be faster."

Emma wouldn't have been as direct. When she saw Greg stiffen, she tried to slouch comfortably against Cole.

"I'm terribly sorry, sir," the steward answered. "As you know, that's not possible at this time."

"Why not?" Cole asked, his tone confrontational.

"Mr. Del Conte's orders."

Cole hesitated, and Emma hoped he wasn't going to press the hired help for information he shouldn't be giving out. And also hoped he wasn't putting them on someone's watch list. Like—the couple most likely to get tossed into the brig if they made any trouble.

To her relief, he dropped the interrogation and reached into his pocket.

When he pulled out his billfold and started to peel off a five, Greg waved his hand. "The staff doesn't accept tips. Mr. Del Conte's orders."

Cole lowered his voice. "Not even for extra services?"

"No, sir. Are you sure I can't get you something to drink?"

Emma's mouth had turned dry, and she moistened her lips as she glanced at Cole. "Sweetie, can I have a soda water with lime?"

He gave her an indulgent smile. "Sure. And I'll take one, too, to keep my honey company."

When the man had departed, Emma let out a sigh.

"Just relax, sweet thing," Cole said. "You're going to love this vacation."

She wanted to tell him to stop with the cute endearments. Instead she said, "You know new places make me a little nervous."

"I'm, sure Mr. Del Conte knows how to make everyone feel at home."

He clicked the button on the remote, and a scene leaped onto the screen.

It showed an empty stage with the curtain drawn.

"That's from one of the theaters on the *Windward*," Greg said, as he set two drinks down on the table. It's recorded so you get the whole performance."

"Thanks," Cole said as he picked up his drink. "How often are there shows."

"You can find something almost every hour."

49

"That's amazing." Emma took a gulp of her own drink to moisten her dry mouth.

"The shows are a highlight for many of our guests. There are several shows you can watch now. Channel one is a dance number," Greg informed them. "Channel two is a dungeon scene. Channel three is a schoolgirl being punished for not learning her lessons. Channel four is . . ."

"The dance number," Cole interrupted.

"Oh, I love dancers," Emma added said.

"I'll leave you to enjoy the performance."

The steward disappeared from view as the lights on the screen brightened. A spotlight swung to the side of the stage, and a couple stepped into it. They both looked to be in their twenties, with lean, athletic builds. The woman wore a halter-top sundress that swirled around her legs. The man wore a short-sleeved shirt and dark slacks.

As *Stranger in Paradise* came softly from the speakers, the man and woman began to dance.

They started with classical ballet moves, but the performance soon became more sexually explicit. When the man lifted his partner up and twirled her above his head, his palm braced itself squarely against her crotch. And when he lowered her, he let her body glide suggestively against his.

Emma tried not to react, but after the emotional strain of the day, she found that the suggestive performance was turning her on.

Cole pulled her close, nuzzling his lips against her ear. "I'm sure they're watching our reactions."

She kept her eyes on the screen, trying to stay steady as the male dancer reached for the tie at the back of his partner's neck. When he undid the knot, she stepped away from him, letting the bodice of the sundress fall to her waist, exposing her high, rounded breasts.

The woman's hands went to her waist, where she undid another tie and tossed the bodice of the dress away.

The man stepped behind her. As they swayed to the music, his hands cupped her breasts while his fingers began to play with her nipples, teasing them to taut peaks as he pulled and twisted them.

Emma caught her breath, embarrassed that her own nipples had tightened as she watched the couple.

The performance could have been crude. But it was all done with extreme sensuality.

The male dancer unfastened his partner's skirt. When she stepped out of it, she was totally naked.

Beside Emma, Cole made a low sound.

Seeing a nude woman didn't excite her, but she couldn't say the same for Cole.

Bruno Del Conte took a sip from the iced latte that a very attractive young woman had brought him.

Leaning back in his comfortable desk chair, he picked up a pile of papers on his desk. It was always fascinating to see how much rich men would pay to visit the *Windward*. And he hadn't done a bit of paid advertising. It was all word of mouth from satisfied customers—many of whom came back every few months to enjoy the unique opportunities he provided.

Of course, most of those guys were rich old perverts who appreciated the liberal policies on Bruno Del Conte's private ocean liner. And the special drug cocktails that helped them get it up. Maybe he was chopping a few years off their lives, but they'd die happy.

He laughed.

The point was, he'd found an excellent way to indulge his own unusual tastes while making money off the men—and a few women—who were glad to pay for his special services.

Which brought him to Cole Mason, who'd booked one of his medium-priced suites at the last minute.

Fairly young, good looking guy. Not the usual kind of man who came to the *Windward*.

He stroked his chin as he read the information his chief of security had printed out for him., then checked his video surveillance equipment, which gave him a direct feed from the lounge on the hovercraft currently bringing Mason to the *Windward*.

Bruno clicked through the screens until he got a view of the sitting area where Mason and his girlfriend were watching a video.

The guy seemed to be enjoying the dance number he was watching. But still, he warranted some further investigation.

As he switched off the video feed, contingencies ran through his mind.

He'd captured the daughter of an enemy. He'd planned to have some fun displaying her to an exclusive group of men this evening, letting them touch her, but nothing more, but maybe that wasn't such a good idea.

Despite its seemingly open appearance, the Tropical Lounge was very secure. There was only one public entrance, and you didn't get in without a special key card. Perhaps it was better to keep her there for the moment. And dig for some more information on Mason.

Meanwhile, he had another problem to deal with. Specifically, a mutiny. Apparently some of his slaves thought they could escape from the ship.

He'd caught and tortured one of the troublemakers, but the man had died before revealing the names of any of his fellows.

CHAPTER SIX

The couple began to dance again, more classical ballet moves, with the woman completely naked, and the man completely dressed—adding to the eroticism of the performance. She came back into his arms and began unbuttoning his shirt. When it was open, she lowered her face to his chest, eagerly licking and sucking at his nipples while her fingers worked the button at the top of his pants, then the zipper.

Emma couldn't drag her eyes from the explicit scene.

Every muscle in her body tightened as the man pressed on the woman's shoulders so that she went down on her knees in front of him. He sank his fingers into her hair, guiding her face to his crotch.

Because of the pants he still wore, Emma couldn't see exactly what she was doing. But it seemed like she was giving him a blow job. He threw his head back, thrusting his hips forward, his face contorted with pleasure.

Lord, how was this going to end?

Next to her, she could hear Cole's harsh breathing. Looking down at his lap, she saw an erection straining against his pants.

She wanted to press her hand over him. She wanted him to cup her breasts. Stroke his fingers against her clit.

But that was only going to make her hotter. She made a small frustrated sound.

"Christ!"

Cole's exclamation broke the spell. Emma looked up, startled to see that their seating area was now completely walled off by a filmy curtain. She'd been so focused on the screen that she hadn't even seen when the curtains had drawn closed.

She looked at Cole, then back at the television. The stage was dark. The man and woman were gone, and she couldn't hold back a laugh.

"What?" Cole demanded.

"We didn't find out whether she made him come."

Cole laughed too. "Yeah. Right."

They stared at each other, and she knew the erotic video had brought them both to the boiling point. Well, not just the video. Eroticism mixed with danger seemed to be a powerful aphrodisiac.

"Emma." He dragged in a breath and let it out before lowering his mouth to hers, taking her startled gasp into his mouth. As his lips moved against hers, one of his hands went to her breast, rubbing back and forth against the tightened peak stabbing against the fabric of her halter top. When she moaned, he worked the other hand into the crotch of her shorts.

"What are you doing," she managed.

"No reason both of us have to suffer."

When she took his meaning, she tried to jerk away, but he held her where she was so that he could slide his hand under her top, teasing her tightened nipple while his other hand began to stroke her intimately.

"Don't," she protested, but not as strongly as she should have. She was hot and wet, and he glided his finger through her sex, up and down, working his way toward her clit and away.

She should make him stop, but she couldn't do it. And when he focused on her clit, she raised her hips to increase the pressure.

You're going to . . ."

"Yeah," he answered, keeping up the maddening stroking, bringing her to a rocketing climax. When she cried out, he drank in her passion.

She lay panting in his arms, shocked to the core by what he had done and what she had let him do when they were on assignment. They had just crossed another line into forbidden territory. Assignment or no.

"You shouldn't have done that," she managed to say.

"I would have stopped, if I'd thought that's what you wanted."

"Cole . . ."

"Let's not argue about it." His voice had taken on a tone she recognized. He was playing the character he'd been assigned, and she'd better play her role as well. "You know I enjoyed myself. I don't get much chance to do that in a setting like this."

"Um." She closed her eyes and leaned against him.

"Is that what this place is like?" she murmured in a barely audible voice.

"Apparently. And more. You heard him reciting the menu of videos. That one was probably one of the milder selections. To get timid customers in the mood."

She'd been in the mood, all right. Now there were a lot of things she wanted to say, but she couldn't mention any of them here. Instead she lay in his arms staring vacantly at the screen thinking that they'd been fighting in the car not so long ago. The erotic performance had changed everything.

Everything?

When the stage lights came up again, Cole snatched up the remote and clicked the power button.

As the television went blank, she breathed out a small sigh. Enough of that.

As Cole slung his arm around her and held her against his side, she heard a change in the engine sound and looked up.

"Must be almost there," he said. "Wow, this is going to be a fun adventure."

"Oh yeah," she managed to agree as he stood again and pulled the curtain back.

Windows ran all around the sides of the hovercraft, and to her right she could see a massive ship. Not as big as some the best known cruise lines were using now, but big enough to make it difficult to find Karen Hopewell.

She saw Cole's eyes narrow and wondered if he was thinking the same thing. Or was he cursing their unprofessional behavior a few moments ago.

Before she could say anything, Greg strode toward them, giving them a broad smile. "We're almost at the *Windward.*"

"An impressive tub," Cole observed.

"Yes. It was a standard cruise ship, but you'll find many modifications inside." He gave them a bright smile. "Did you enjoy the performance?"

"Yeah. But I missed the end. Did she make him come?" Cole asked.

"Yes."

"I'd think it would be difficult to dance with a hard-on like that."

"Our professional performers are all quite disciplined. The amateurs are different, of course. But that's part of the charm."

"Amateurs?" Cole asked.

"Yes. Some of our guests are inspired to take part in performances. And some of the girls here are just learning professional moves."

Emma looked down at her hands. "Oh."

Cole had warned her about something like that, but she hadn't really believed him.

"You'll be entering the ship at Deck Three. Your room is on Deck Five. We'll have your luggage brought up."

Emma felt a cold shiver go through her. This was it. They were stepping into Bruno Del Conte's lair, and there was no going back.

Greg was speaking again. "Because we want to maintain strict security for our guests, our entry procedures are rather rigid. Would you please turn in your cell phones and any other communications devices you've brought."

"We left our phones in our hotel room," Cole said.

Greg looked annoyed but said nothing.

A hatch in the side of the ship had opened, and a gangway lowered, connecting to an exit from the hovercraft opposite where they had entered.

Cole took her arm and ushered her across, and they stepped into a small room with thick carpeting, expensive artwork on the paneled walls, and two men wearing the same uniform as Greg. A woman dressed in an exotic blue and green sari stood behind them.

"Welcome to the *Windward*," one of the men said. He was tall, with a completely bald head and bulging muscles. Could he have been one of the goons who'd kidnapped Karen? Not much to go on, but it was possible. Someone from Baltimore would probably have stayed with her.

The other man was blond and also muscular. The woman was tiny and exotic looking with olive skin and large dark eyes.

They all wore name tags. The two men were Jed and Ames. The woman was Sahadra.

"We need to do a security check before you enter," Jed said. He looked at Cole. "Empty your pockets and step through the metal detector." To Emma, he said, "Put your purse on the table and step through after Mr. Mason.

She did as he requested, watching as Ames did a pat down of Cole. It was like one of those thorough searches at the airport where they run their hands up your legs into your crotch.

Sahadra spoke, and Emma's attention snapped to her. "I must pat you down as well. Please hold your hands out to the sides.

When Emma complied, the woman began to pat her down, cupping her breasts, stroking her fingers across the nipples.

"Is that necessary?" Emma asked.

"We have to be careful about who comes on board." She slid her hands down Emma's ribs, across her middle, then down to her crotch. Emma gritted her teeth, willing herself not to sock the woman. She was just doing her job. Or was she going all out with the intimate touching because it gave her a thrill? "We have a strict policy about drugs."

Yeah, you've got to buy them on the ship, not bring your own, Emma thought, but she kept the observation to herself.

The frisking was almost finished when she heard loud voices and some kind of scuffle out of sight down the hall.

The woman turned in alarm, just as the sound of shots rang out.

CHAPTER SEVEN

Sahadra pushed Emma to the floor. As she tried to scramble up, the man named Jed drew his gun and held it on Emma and Cole.

The other man, Ames, also drew a gun, but he turned and ran rapidly out of the room, disappearing from sight down a bend in the hall.

"Stay here," Jed growled as Sahadra backed up and joined him. She was also holding a weapon that must have been hidden under the folds of her sari. She looked alarmed but also determined.

Emma stared at them, shocked by how quickly the whole situation had changed from an annoying pat down to something much more dangerous.

She waited tensely for the gunfire to come closer, wondering what she was going to do? Make a grab for Sahadra's gun?

But the shooting stopped as quickly as it had begun. In the aftermath, she could hear people shouting and screaming. She would have gone to help, but it was clear that the man and woman guarding them wouldn't let her or Cole see what was happening.

She looked toward Cole, who was also on the deck, his face a study in tension, his body coiled to spring.

Lord, what if Cole did something that could get him killed?

That terrible thought made her realize what she'd been trying to deny. It wasn't just lust between them. She cared about him with a strength that shocked her.

Moving slowly, she reached toward him, putting a steadying hand on his arm.

When his head swung toward her, their eyes met.

"Stay with me," she whispered, hoping that bringing herself into the equation would keep him from doing anything dangerous now.

He took a deep breath and let it out, then nodded, and she saw he was making an effort to calm down.

As the seconds ticked by, she looked back toward the entrance hatch. It was still open, and she could see the hovercraft racing away.

Movement in the doorway caught her attention. A man they hadn't met before strode into the room. His name tag said he was Ben. He was about six feet tall with dark hair, dark eyes and a commanding presence. Emma would bet that he had some kind of authority on the ship.

"All clear," he said.

Sahadra tucked her weapon back into her sari. Jed reholstered his gun under his jacket.

"Sorry about that," he said to the arriving guests.

"What happened?" Cole demanded.

"Just a minor disturbance," the man answered, his voice conveying that he wasn't giving out any information.

But Cole didn't take the hint. "Then why did you hold us at gunpoint?"

"To make sure you didn't get hurt."

"By what?"

"We were taking precautions."

"But you gave the all clear. So let us in on the news."

Ben kept his gaze steady. "We use some large cats in some of our acts. One of them got out."

"And you shot him?"

"No. We shot at him—with blanks. He was frightened and ran back to the animal area. We have him under control. Everything's okay. I'm sorry that the incident marred your arrival. To make amends, I'm authorized to upgrade you to one of our most desirable suites."

"That's big of you," Cole said, his voice tight.

Emma was pretty sure he wanted to say a lot more, but he wisely refrained from needling the guy further.

That couldn't stop her speculations. Was this really about an animal escaping? Or were they actually shooting at people? And why?

"Let me show you to the suite," Ben said, cutting off the question and answer session. Turning, he stepped out of the reception area.

Cole reached for Emma's hand, as they followed him. Ames brought up the rear. An escort? Or a guard detail to make sure they didn't stray from the approved route?

She kept her gaze down, trying to look submissive as she inspected the carpet.

When she saw a large, fresh stain that she thought was a pool of blood, she stopped short.

Cole followed her gaze, then tugged on her hand.

She started walking again, seeing more droplets of blood on the wall.

Which meant that at least part of Ben's explanation was a lie. They hadn't shot at an animal with blanks. They had shot and wounded or killed it. Or perhaps it wasn't an animal. Did they really have big cats on the boat? And how would one have gotten out?

Ben escorted them to an elevator that was bigger than she'd seen in many apartment buildings. Their original room was supposed to be on Deck Five, but the suite was two levels higher.

When they reached Deck Seven, he turned right, leading them down a corridor.

"You're in the front of the ship," he said. "With a magnificent view."

Bending, he swiped a key card in a reader, and the door opened.

Emma had been in ships' cabins before, but nothing as luxurious as *this*. They stepped into a living room furnished with comfortable contemporary sofas and tables. Beyond she could see a large bedroom where their bags rested on two wooden luggage racks.

Ben led them through, showing them an enormous bathroom with a double marble sink counter, a tub and a shower. The toilet was in a separate little room. But she was hardly taking any of it in. She was too shaken by the shooting incident and the implications. And by her feelings for Cole that she could no longer repress.

"The book on the desk will give you the layout of the ship and tell you what you need to know about the *Windward*. We have regular seatings in the dining room, but you can order room service any time. And there are several casual restaurants in various locations. You can also have room service in any of the playrooms. Do you have any questions?" he asked as though he were a bellman in a luxury hotel—instead of someone who was obviously on the security staff.

Unable to rein in her emotions, Emma blurted, "We'd like to be alone now."

"Of course," he answered, switching gears immediately. "I'll just leave your key cards on the desk." He set down two cards, then turned and strode toward the door to the suite.

Cole followed him, waiting until he was outside before closing and locking the door.

When he came back to Emma, she melted into his arms.

"He's lying," she whispered. She was about to speculate about his role on the ship when Cole shook his head.

"Yeah, but let's not talk about it," he said, a warning note in his voice, and she realized that she'd forgotten the conversation in the car about microphones. That seemed like a thousand years ago. When they'd been in the normal world. Not this place that had turned deadly almost as soon a they'd stepped on board.

She was sure someone had been killed. But who and why?

When she made a choking sound, Cole tightened his arms around her, running his hands up and down her back.

He was the only thing she could cling to in a universe that had gone mad.

"That was frightening," she murmured, sure that any normal female guest would have a similar reaction. If she were free to get off this boat, she'd turn around and leave. But they had a job to do. And now it seemed even more urgent than when they'd been given the assignment.

"The security staff took care of it right away. Let's forget it and have fun here," Cole said, putting a note of bravado in his voice.

Oh sure.

She held tight to him, needing him, in so many ways. More than she could name. But she understood where she was going to start.

And she knew on some deep, instinctive level that it was the same for him. Heat flared between them. The same heat they had felt earlier. Still he tried to pull away.

"Don't," he choked out.

She kept her voice low. "I won't let you push me away because you think it's the right thing to do."

"It is."

"You're wrong, and I can prove it."

They had reached the end of the conversation. Moving one hand upward, she cupped her palm around the back of his head and brought his mouth down to hers.

They had kissed before, with an urgency that had taken her breath away. On the hovercraft, he had brought her to climax after they'd watched the erotic dance. All of that was nothing to what she felt now.

Need coursed through her. Not just arousal. Need for *this man*. All of him, not just what he had given her a little while earlier.

The feel of his mouth on hers sent hot, urgent messages to every one of her nerve endings.

And when she heard him make a low sound of surrender, she felt joy leap in her chest—in her soul.

His mouth turned rapacious as he drank from her like a man who had been denied water for an eternity.

In response, she opened for him, eager to give him anything he wanted—and at the same time take what *she* needed.

Strong forces had been building between them for eons, maybe since the first day they'd met, and the dangers of this place had brought it all into sharp, aching focus.

She swayed against him, hardly able to stand on her own.

"You're sure?" he murmured.

"Oh yes."

He raised his head and looked around. "Someone could be watching."

"Oh Lord. I . . ."

With a growl, he picked her up in his arms and carried her to the bed. Still holding her, he bent to sweep the covers back.

After laying her on the cool sheets, he strode back to the door and flipped the light switch, plunging the room into darkness except for a shaft of light coming from the bathroom.

He took care of that by closing the door almost all the way, leaving only the barest sliver of light. She heard him kick off his shoes before he came down on the bed beside her, gathering her in his arms again.

She knew that he had fought the feelings building between them, and he had lost the capacity to keep fighting. Maybe back on the hovercraft he could pretend he was simply being chivalrous. Not now.

"Shit." Bruno Del Conte stared at the black monitor screen. That bastard Mason had turned off the lights, just when things were getting interesting. So did he know that someone might be watching? Did he have inside information, or was he just being cautious.

Leaning over, Bruno fiddled with the brightness, but it didn't help.

A knock on the door made him sit back in his chair.

"Come in," he called.

His security chief, Ben Walker, entered. Walker had been with him for the past six months. He was good man, meticulous, quick to crack down on troublemakers, and able to pretend that he was only a minor player on the security team.

"What happened down there exactly?"

"A slave found out the hovercraft was due and tried to escape."

"How did he think he was getting on board?"

"He had a crew member's uniform."

"Which he got how?"

"Maybe from the laundry."

"And what happened to him?"

"They challenged him before he got to the embarkation area. He ran, and they shot him. He's dead."

"Good."

"I'm sorry for the disturbance. It seems that the unrest has spread farther than we originally thought. I'll be personally reviewing the sex sessions that included the dead man."

"What's his name?"

"Joseph Naguro."

"I can't remember anything special about him."

In the five years he'd been operating the *Windward*, Bruno had had problems from time to time, but never at such a sustained level. It was as though people who should know their place were thinking they deserved unwarranted consideration.

"Do you think Cole Mason and Emma Ray have anything to do with it?"

"I think they were at the wrong place at the wrong time."

"Maybe. What were your impressions of them?"

"He kept his cool in a tense situation." He laughed. "Well, he got a little smart aleck in his remarks."

"How do you interpret that?"

"His response to being pushed to the floor and having a gun held on him."

"Was he in danger?" Bruno snapped.

"If the rebels had gotten into the reception area, he would have been."

"Maybe we didn't check out Mason carefully enough. Go over his background. And Ms. Ray's. I mean more than what we've already got."

"Yes sir. Is there anything else you need at the moment."

"I think we've covered it," Bruno answered. When his security chief left, he repressed the urge to pick up the glass on his desk and throw it at the bulkhead. But that would make a mess someone would have to clean up, and he didn't want anyone to know he was upset by this latest incident.

He looked around his office, loving the furnishings and artwork he'd picked out. The juggler across from his desk was a genuine Picasso etching. The huge abstract on the sidewall was a Jackson Pollock. And he'd taken a very nice Salvador Dali from his father's collection.

He'd outfitted this ship for his own pleasure and turned it into as close to a kingdom as you could get without being born into royalty. Now some of his subjects were trying to fuck that all up.

He grimaced, then pressed a button that brought up a flat-screen TV on the far side of the desk. He had a library of tapes that always soothed him. He'd watch one now.

Rather than tie one of his slaves to the whipping post. Another decision not to give anything away.

Relatively few people in the world knew who he was and how he had gotten where he was today. Those who did thought he had always had it made. But it hadn't started out so well. Bruno had been sickly as a child. He'd eaten a lot of bananas trying to keep everything he ate from going through him. Just as his digestion had gotten better, he'd started school and turned out to be a slow learner. He'd needed endless tutoring just to get the hang of reading. His older brother Dieter had been robust and quick at his studies, and his parents' favorite son.

He'd ached for what his brother had. The good health. The easy time in school. His charm. He'd used all of those to get what he wanted, and it had looked like he'd succeeded.

Until he'd screwed up in his early twenties, driven drunk, and plowed his Mercedes into a lady crossing the street. Papa's money hadn't kept him out of jail for manslaughter. And Bruno had used those two years to prove he was the model son. Dieter had come back from his prison term angry at the injustice of what had happened. And angry when he saw he'd lost his place as the favorite. Which had only worsened his position.

Papa had bent over backwards to be fair. He'd left his two sons the same inheritance. But Papa had drawn closer to Bruno, given him good advice. Which he'd taken. And prospered.

For all his early promise, Dieter had never done anything important on his own. In fact he'd made some very bad investments. Bruno had pretended sympathy and been glad to bail him out when he'd been secretly gleeful that his brother had made a mess of things. Instead of succeeding—through hard work and guts.

After dragging his thoughts away from the past, Bruno scrolled through his private film library and found one of his

favorites. Called Marlene. A woman forced to service a series
of men.

In the darkness, Emma felt Cole's hands working the ties
of her halter top before tossing it onto the floor.

Her own hands were no less busy as she pulled his shirt
over his head, then fumbled for the button at the top of his
slacks.

She wanted to experience this with all her senses,
including sight, but she understood why he had darkened
the room. It was the only way to make sure they had some
privacy.

She ached to say so many things, but she would have to
communicate in other ways. Like Morse code, only better.

When he slipped his hands into her panties and cupped
the rounded curve of her ass, she felt her sex go hot and
slick. When he dipped lower, sliding a hand into her cleft, she
went up in flames.

His fingers glided through the slick wetness, dipping into
her, circling the entrance to her vagina. Teasing her there
before stroking upward to her clit.

As he felt her reaction, he made a sound of approval, low
in his throat.

He leaned down to take one of her distended nipples into
his mouth, sucking hard, wringing a glad cry from her lips.

She found the band at the top of his shorts, tugging them
down so that his cock sprang out as she freed it.

He kicked his pants off the end of the bed. Naked, he
gathered her close, stroking his fingers over her back, down
her flanks, pulling her against his body.

As they rocked together on the bed, she wondered why
they didn't set the sheets on fire.

"Now, please now," she whispered.

"Not yet. I want you molten."

"I am."

Easing away, he took her breasts in his hands, his thumbs stroking over the hardened tips, making her whimper with need as she arched into the caress.

He used his mouth on her again, this time teasing one pebble hard nipple with his tongue and teeth while he used his thumb and finger on its mate.

If he waited much longer to finish this, she would lose her mind. Reaching down, she closed her hand around his erection, feeling the size and weight of him, then moving her hand up and down, squeezing tightly.

He made a low, ragged sound.

"Time to feel you inside me," she gasped.

With a growl, he rolled her to her back, clasping her to him, and she guided him into her.

They both cried out at the joining. She wanted to look into his eyes. She wanted to tell him how much she had secretly craved this, even when she couldn't even admit it to herself.

Now she wanted to say that they belonged together—until the end of time.

But she couldn't say it. This was too new—and unexpected. All she could do was cling to him as he moved within her, fast then faster taking her up and up to where the air was almost too thin to breathe. When he reached between them, pressing a finger against her clit, she felt her inner muscles tighten around him, the contractions like small electric shocks that spread from her sex to the rest of her body.

And as an all consuming orgasm still gripped her, she felt release grab him. Throwing his head back, he shouted out his pleasure.

She was shaken to the depths of her soul as he collapsed against her, his head drifting to her shoulder.

Knowing that her whole life had changed, she reached to stroke her fingers through his hair, then turned to softly kiss his cheek.

He shifted to his side, and they lay clasping each other for long moments. When he reached for her hand, she knit her fingers with his.

For a while Cole had carried her away to a land where only the two of them existed. But as they lay together in the darkness, Emma remembered exactly where they were. And why.

No matter how desperately she wanted to get away from this place, they had a job to do, and they couldn't leave until they had finished it.

"Hell of a time for this," he muttered.

"Um." She nodded against his shoulder, fighting the need to bombard him with questions. Was he simply reacting to the tension of the situation? Or what?

He brought his mouth to her ear. "We can't stay here too long. We've got to go out and explore—like we're super excited to be in this wonderful playground."

"I know," she answered, although she wanted to stay where she was, safe in his arms.

"Did you say you wanted to go to the beauty salon?" he said in a louder voice. "And some of the clothing boutiques?"

". Right."

Forcing herself to roll away from him, she stood up and walked to the bathroom where she shrugged into one of the soft terry robes hanging on the wall.

Cole dragged in a breath and let it out as he watched Emma disappear into the bathroom. He would have liked to follow her. Tempting images of his climbing into the shower and making love to her all over again flashed through his mind.

Much as he wanted to pull her naked body against himself, he was glad of the chance to be alone for a few minutes. He'd told himself that he wasn't going to make love to her, which had been total bullshit. Of course he'd been going to. The need for her had been building inside him like an atomic explosion. On the hovercraft, he hadn't been able to keep his hands off her. And just now, he'd gone over the edge like a rutting stag.

Which was all wrong for their relationship. He should have been tender with her. He should have had the luxury of some private time with her before she found out she had bonded to a werewolf.

Too bad he couldn't ask for some advice from another one of the Marshall clan. But he couldn't send an e-mail from here. And they'd probably wonder who the hell he was if he did. He'd stayed away from his family, too. He knew that some of his cousins had gotten together and formed a pack or something like that. The idea had made him cringe. He was the alpha male in his own damn pack. And he wasn't taking orders from anyone.

On the other hand, he hadn't heard of any Marshall werewolves killing each other. Which must mean they'd worked out some kind of arrangement.

Could he fit in with them? Did he want to?

Maybe for Emma's sake. He knew his mom still led an isolated, miserable life as the wife of a dominant lone wolf who made his living as a real estate agent so he could come and go as he pleased. And occasionally rob houses that he knew were vacant.

His parents relationship had been part of his reason for trying to avoid bonding. He hadn't wanted to fall into the trap of treating another woman the way his father had treated his mother.

But he wasn't his father. He'd proved that to himself by going to college and getting a degree in criminal justice, before joining Decorah Security.

Still, he was feeling more confused about his personal life than he ever had. And he had the terrible suspicion that Emma was going to find out his big secret under the worst possible conditions.

He cursed under his breath, mindful of the listening devices that were probably registering everything that went on in this room—and everywhere else on the ship.

Thank God they—and Emma—couldn't listen in on his thoughts.

By the time Emma returned to the bedroom wearing one of the robes she'd found in the bathroom, Cole had pulled on the clothing he'd been wearing and was sitting at the desk looking through some of the *Windward* materials.

He kept his eyes on the printed material.

"I've been reading about the activities here. While you're checking out the girly stuff, I'll do some exploring on my own."

"Yes. We should find out what we can do on the ship," Emma murmured, trying to sound enthusiastic. "But I haven't even checked out this room yet." She walked to the drapes and pulled them open. Outside was a balcony which was only a little smaller than the one at Karen's apartment. She pulled open the sliding glass door and stepped out, feeling the wind in her hair. At the sides of the balcony were metal walls that made it impossible to see the rooms on either side. The only view was straight ahead, showing a vista of blue ocean and sky.

Walking to the rail, she felt the wind ruffling her hair. When she looked down, she saw the water far below. What if the only way to get out of here was to jump? Would she survive?

She shuddered, putting the thought out of her mind.

Footsteps alerted her that she wasn't alone. Cole came up beside her and slipped his arm around her shoulder.

She cut him a sideways look. She'd always been attracted to him. Always thought of him as a handsome guy. Now he was *her guy.*

Maybe. Neither of them had planned the intimacy that had exploded between them, but it was the two ton elephant in the room. Unfortunately, it wasn't something they could deal with now. Any real discussion between them would have to wait until they got off the ship.

And then what?

Don't think about the future, she ordered herself. You'll have to deal with that when life is back to normal again. Or would it ever be what she'd considered normal? What about Cole's dysfunctional family? When he shared it with her, would that influence her decision about the two of them?

"Look at that view," he said aloud.

"Nothing to see but water and sky."

"Yeah. That's what I mean. We've left the real world, and we've got nothing to do but enjoy ourselves."

"Right," she agreed, fighting to put enthusiasm into her voice, since they probably had microphones here, too."

He waited a beat before asking, "You ever made love outside?"

"No."

"We ought to try it later." He looked at the walls on either side of them. "I mean, nobody can see us."

"Um."

Who was speaking, she wondered. The man who had made love to her or the agent on assignment? Was he thinking he could climb down and get to some other part of the ship. Or was he just trying to project the character he was supposed to be? She had never been more confused about a relationship or more frustrated by the inability to speak openly.

Before she could respond, he turned and went back inside. She stayed at the rail for a few more minutes.

When she came back to the stateroom, he had changed into a fresh shirt and slacks. "Let's meet back here in a couple of hours," he said.

"How much can I spend in the boutique?"

"As much as you want on clothing. And costume jewelry's okay. But don't buy any gold or diamonds unless you consult me first. The last time I turned you loose, you went a little crazy."

"Sorry."

He headed for the door, leaving her alone in the bedroom where she quickly dressed in one of the outfits from the suitcase.

After checking the book with the layout of the ship, she slipped out of the room, feeling her heart pound. She didn't like this place and didn't like being alone, but she wasn't going to let that stop her.

As she walked down the hall to the elevator, she passed a muscular brunette woman carrying a gym bag walking briskly down the hall. Incongruously, she was wearing a short robe and stiletto heels that clicked on the tile floor. She stopped at a stateroom door and knocked. A man came to the door wearing only a towel around his waist. His bare chest and shoulders were crisscrossed with red slash lines, and he had an eager expression on his face.

Emma couldn't stop herself from staring at him.

He looked her up and down, then grinned. "Want to join us?"

Her mouth was so dry she could hardly speak. "No."

"Did you come here with your boyfriend?"

She shouldn't answer. She should just keep walking, but she heard herself say, "Yes."

"He's off having his own fun. So you can do what you want, right?"

She took a step back.

"Bonnie will show you a good time."

"No thanks."

When she turned and hurried away, she heard his laughter echoing after her.

The sound of the door closing made her grimace. She didn't want to think about what the couple were going to do in there, much less join them, but she couldn't stop vivid pictures from running through her mind.

She took the elevator to Deck Three, stepped out, and looked at the sign that gave directions.

The beauty salon was in one direction and the clothing boutiques were in the other.

She hated shopping, and the beauty salon was her main target, so she headed in that direction.

When she stepped inside the mauve and silver waiting room, she was confronted by two women in black uniforms, both wearing name tags. One was a delicate Asian beauty named Anna. The other was a willowy blond named Allison.

"Can I help you?" the blond asked.

Emma paused to get her bearings. She couldn't be sure why, but there seemed to be an undercurrent of tension between the two *Windward* employees. Because they disliked working together? Or because they didn't trust each other?

An older woman came out of the bathroom, wearing a smock.

"I'm ready for my pedicure," she said in a commanding voice.

"Certainly, Ms. Davis," Allison answered.

She and Anna exchanged glances before she ushered the woman into a private room and closed the door.

Anna turned back to Emma with an inquiring look on her face. "Can I have your name?"

"Emma Ray."

She scanned a computer screen on the counter. "You don't have an appointment."

"Oh, I'm sorry. I didn't realize I needed one. I just thought . . ."

"We may be able to work you in."

"What services do you perform?"

The woman handed her a glossy brochure, and she scanned the list—that included standard haircuts and color applications, complete with stunning examples of women with hair and makeup done to perfection. She also saw that she could ask for some unusual services like body piercing or even tattooing.

Improvising on the spur of the moment, she asked in a tentative voice, "Could I have my pubic hair shaved?"

The beautician didn't blink. "Of course."

"You're experienced with that?" Emma pressed. "I wouldn't want anything important to get cut."

Anna gave her a reassuring smile. "I assure you, you're in good hands."

Emma looked around the waiting area. "Where do you do it?"

"In here." Anna led the way into a private room with a table similar to a doctor's office.

"I've never had that done before," Emma confided. "It's kind of making me nervous to think about someone using a razor down there." She cleared her throat, "but my boyfriend said he'd like to see me that way."

"There's nothing to be worried about. Many women enjoy the look. It's youthful. And a lot of men find it sexually stimulating."

Emma examined the room's setup, then looked down at the floor. Near the end of the table she saw a few curls of red hair, and her pulse picked up. That could be Karen's hair. There was no way to tell for sure without a DNA analysis, but how many people had that striking color?

Anna followed her gaze and drew in a quick breath. "Oh, I'm so sorry," she said. "It looks like this room wasn't cleaned properly this morning. I'll speak to the staff."

"That's all right," Emma answered. "You did someone recently?"

"Yes," the beautician murmured.

Before Emma could ask another question, they were interrupted by a loud knock at the door. They both looked up in surprise as Cole stepped into the room.

"What are you doing here?" Emma asked, genuinely startled by his unexpected appearance in the beauty salon.

He sounded a little breathless, like he'd been hurrying to find her. "I'm glad I knew where you were going. I was just getting into a private consultation with one of the entertainment directors when I got a message that Mr. Del Conte would like us to join him for dinner."

CHAPTER EIGHT

Emma tried to take that in. Del Conte was going to socialize with them? Because he suspected something? Or because he was making an effort to cultivate new arrivals to his private paradise?

"But I thought we were going to have some fun this evening," she murmured. As she spoke, she moved her foot, poking at the red hair she'd noticed on the floor in the treatment room and saw Cole follow her gaze.

Although he didn't outwardly react, she was pretty sure he'd seen what she was pointing out. As though oblivious to anything besides the news he'd come to deliver, he said, "I wanted to find you right away. An invitation from Mr. Del Conte is special."

"What time is dinner?"

"Seven."

Emma glanced at her watch. That gave them only an hour and a half before the command performance.

"That's so exciting," she answered, making her voice sound like a little girl who had just gotten a pony for birthday. She looked at Anna as though the woman hadn't just heard Cole's announcement. "Mr. Del Conte has invited us to have dinner with him. That's such an honor. I didn't expect that kind of personal attention when we booked this cruise."

Anna gave Cole a brilliant smile. "You must be an important guest."

"I don't know about that," he allowed acting like a bigwig who was struggling to seem modest.

Emma went with her ditz brain girlfriend impersonation. "You're rich," she burbled. "He respects that."

Anna nodded. "You have some time before dinner. Emma told me you'd like to have her intimate areas shaved, but she's a little nervous about it because she's never tried it before. Do you want me to do it now? You might like to watch."

"I don't think we have time to do it right. Maybe later," Cole answered easily.

"Yes, of course."

"I think we'll go back to our room and get ready."

Emma felt like she'd just been granted a reprieve, but when he didn't move, she wondered what he was up to now.

Anna gave him an inquiring look.

He cleared his throat. "I guess you're an expert on the *Windward*. Do a lot of the men like the look of a shaved pussy?" he asked.

"I don't comment on the guests' tastes," Anna said stiffly.

"Yeah, but between you and me, I'd like to get a feel for the vibes here."

"There are no vibes. Really anything goes."

"You've been part of scenarios?"

"Yes."

"And you work on slaves, too?"

Anna looked even more uncomfortable. "We don't talk about that."

"I guess the rules are different in the beauty salon. I was getting acquainted with some of the services. Stuff I hadn't even thought of. Like my facilitator was saying that Emma could be part of a slave market with women presented for my selection. Or I could have my mark tattooed on her if I wanted." He paused and dropped his voice. "Some men even have it done as a brand. With the woman chained to a post."

Emma couldn't hold back a gasp.

"I haven't made up my mind," he said. "We'll talk about it later."

"Do I get a say?" she snapped.

He reached out and stroked his finger against her cheek. "That depends on how much you want to please me."

Bruno Del Conte kept his voice even and his hands at his sides, but he knew he wasn't fooling his senior security officer. Something was amiss on the *Windward*, and his temper was threatening to boil over.

"What have you found out about Joseph Naguro?" he asked.

"He was here as a slave—on a one-year contract. He had three more months to go. He could swing either way—straight or gay."

"You looked at all his scenes?"

"Well, some of it on fast forward. He was in demand by a lot of clients."

"Did some of the action get too rough for him?"

"Maybe not for him. He might have been reacting to conditions for some of the women."

"Such as?"

Walker shifted from one foot to the other. "There were three deaths among the female staffers who had contact with him. We do try to keep that quiet, but word apparently leaked out to cast members."

"Okay. I want any troublemakers brought directly to me."

"Yes, sir."

"What have you found out about Ms. Ray?"

"I thought it was more important to background Naguro first."

In the hallway, Emma kept her head down and spoke in a low voice, playing the part of the woman who was here as Cole Mason's girlfriend.

"I came here because I thought it would be fun. You're starting to spook me with that slave market and branding stuff."

"Just relax, honey," he said with an edge in his voice, and she wondered exactly where this was going.

"You saw the hair in the treatment room?" she said in a barely audible voice.

"Yeah," he muttered and kept walking.

"And what did you smell?"

His head swung toward her, then away.

"What I expected to smell."

"Okay."

In the room, he headed straight for the shower, leaving her to get ready for the evening.

She sat down at the dressing table. She'd never spent a lot of time on hair and makeup, but she'd gotten some inspiration from the pictures she'd seen in the beauty salon.

She swept her hair up, fastening it with combs she found in her luggage, then tackled the makeup that had also been packed for her, applying eye shadow, liner, color base and blusher. Then she polished her nails.

Cole emerged from the bathroom and started getting ready. "I hope Del Conte doesn't expect us to dress up for dinner," he muttered as he inspected himself in the full-length mirror.

"This is a fun-type cruise," she answered. "It's got to be informal."

Cole had been trying to distance himself from Emma, but when she spoke, he glanced up, then almost lost the ability to breathe. Usually her appearance was no nonsense, but she'd put on a white sundress that cupped her breasts and clung to her hips in a way that made him want to rip the damn thing off of her and throw her onto the bed.

She'd also applied makeup he'd never imagined her wearing and painted her nails bright red, showed him a side of her he hadn't seen before.

When she caught his expression, she flushed. They stared at each other for long moments, and he knew that if they didn't get out of the room soon, they were going to miss the big dinner.

Quickly he checked his watch. "Time to go."

"Will I do?" she prodded.

"You know you will," he snapped, then headed for the door.

He'd studied the maps of the ship. When they stepped out of their room, he led her down the corridor to the elevator, which they took to Deck Five.

Tough looking men who seemed more like bouncers than an honor guard stood on either side of the elevator door when they stepped out.

"Just a moment," one of them said. "Can I see your room key?"

Cole handed over his room key card, and the guard ran it through some kind of scanner.

"Thank you, Mr. Mason," he said. He tipped his head toward Emma. 'Ms. Ray."

"Kind of strict security," Cole murmured. "Do you ever relax and have fun?"

"Sorry for the inconvenience," the man answered. "Right this way to the owner's dining room."

He hadn't realized they were eating in a separate room.

When Emma gave him a questioning look, he took her arm, ushering her to a doorway where another guard stood.

The room beyond was pretty large for a private dining room. In fact, it was more like a supper club—with only one round table that seated eight. It was at the left side of the room, leaving a large space in front of a thirty-foot wide stage.

"Fancy," Emma breathed as they stepped through the door. Two couples stood in the general vicinity of the table. Cole studied them. One of the men was short and pudgy and accompanied by a breathtakingly beautiful blond. The other man was taller and fitter. His companion was a beautiful light-skinned black woman.

The two men were eying Cole and Emma. The women kept their gazes fixed on their companions.

A dark-haired hostess came walking toward the newcomers, carrying a tray of champagne flutes and wearing a black dress that barely covered her ass.

Cole glanced at her, then did a double take. The top of her bodice cradled the bottom of her creamy breasts, pushing them up and thrusting them forward.

He'd seen revealing outfits like that before, but the centers of the woman's breasts had always been covered. In this case, her erect nipples were front and center, pointing toward him. It might have been a turn-on under other circumstances. Like if he hadn't been standing next to the woman who was his lifemate. Even if she didn't know it yet.

From the corner of his eye, he caught her shock.

"Champagne?" the hostess asked, positioning the tray so that her breasts projected out onto it.

Emma swallowed. "Thank you," she managed as she took a flute.

"Well, that was startling," Cole said when the woman had departed.

"Uh huh," was about all she could manage.

Cole watched the other two men in the room as the hostess glided toward them. It was clear that they liked the little sideshow.

The pudgy guy reached to take a glass, brushing his hand against the woman's breast. She smiled at him, kept smiling as he closed his fingers around her nipple, tugging and twisting.

The woman next to him gave a nervous laugh.

Beside Cole, Emma dragging in a startled breath. He reached down to clasp her hand, steadying both of them. Every time he thought he understood this place, something else happened to shake him up. And if that was true for him, it must be doubly true for Emma.

One thing for sure, Bruno Del Conte was perfectly comfortable making the rules here. This was his kingdom, and if he wanted nipples poking at the champagne flutes, he could have them. And if he could treat the hired help in such a demeaning way, what could he do to a woman who was being held captive?

Unpleasant possibilities flew through Cole's mind, and he tried to focus on something else. No point in getting worked up when he could do nothing about Karen Hopewell right now.

To their right a hidden door opened, and a man and woman stepped into the dining room. Cole knew at once that it was Del Conte himself—with a companion who looked like she came from a Middle Eastern country. Or perhaps she was a native American. It was difficult to tell with her eyes so heavily made up.

Their host was tall and good looking, with a shock of silver hair and a lion-like command of the room. Everyone there could be his prey, although Cole judged that some of them weren't smart enough to know it.

"Thank you for joining me," he said, like they'd had a choice.

Apparently, not everyone was as reluctant as Cole and Emma to indulge their host.

"A privilege," the pudgy guy gushed. "I've wanted to come here for a long time. And it's an honor to be invited to the captain's table."

"I hope we're living up to your expectations," Del Conte said, his voice smooth as the sea on a calm day.

"Oh yes. Definitely. I loved that science fiction scenario. That alien female was something else"

"I'm so glad you enjoyed it. We should introduce ourselves. I'm Bruno Del Conte." He gestured toward the woman beside him. "And this is my companion, Maya."

"Henry Davis," the fat guy says. "And I'm renting out Vivian here."

The woman he was "renting" kept her face impassive.

The taller man was Stewart Battle, although Cole thought that might be an alias. The woman with him was Ivy Edwards.

Cole and Emma introduced themselves.

"Shall we sit down," Del Conte suggested.

They arranged themselves around the table, and Cole was unhappy to discover that Del Conte placed himself next to Emma. Which meant that he was interested in her. Or he wanted information. Either choice was a problem.

A waiter came in with a tray holding plates of salad. He was a good-looking black man, naked except for a loincloth.

He courteously set down the plates, then offered guests a choice of dressings.

Werewolves didn't eat much salad, but Cole asked for Thousand Island dressing. Emma made the same selection.

Del Conte took a bite of lettuce, then said, "I like to dine with different guests. Get to know the people who avail themselves of the *Windward*. This is a place where you can indulge any fantasy you'd like to explore."

Cole saw Henry lick his lips. Stewart's face took on a speculative look.

Del Conte ate some more salad. His guests followed suit, and Cole choked down a few bites, pushing the rest around his plate.

Del Conte tipped his head toward Cole. "How did you hear about us?"

"From an old college buddy."

"One of our previous guests?"

"Yes." Cole named a guy who had been mentioned in the briefing book, hoping Del Conte wasn't going to check the reference. Or perhaps that had been taken care of along with the rest of his cover story.

The *Windward*'s owner turned to Emma. "I'm so pleased that Cole brought you here."

She swallowed.

Before she could speak, Cole cut in, "We're a couple."

"Which means what, exactly?" their host pressed.

"That we're together—exclusively."

"You don't like watching her with another woman?"

"No."

"With another man?"

"No."

Del Conte looked at them inquiringly. "Then what brought you to the *Windward*?"

"We were planning on having some fun together," Cole answered, struggling to keep his voice even. "I'm sure you have equipment and settings we won't find anywhere else."

"Undoubtedly. What do you like in particular?"

"The ancient world."

"Greek and Roman slaves?"

"Yeah, and Druid," he answered, just for the fun of it. He knew Emma was sitting rigidly beside him, holding her fork in a death grip.

"And you sent Emma to the beauty salon to have her pussy shaved. It might be more fun to make it part of a scenario."

"Like what?"

"Well, suppose you were doing a medieval scene. She could be accused as a witch and dragged off to a prison cell. You'd be the inquisitor. Back then, they shaved off all the hair of the accused women so that they could look for witch marks." He smiled. "Of course, discipline fits very well into that scenario."

Cole stroked his chin. "Hum. I guess I never thought of that."

Beside him, Emma sucked in a sharp breath, her gaze going from Cole to Del Conte.

Before Del Conte could make another clever suggestion, the lights flickered out, then came on again, and Cole saw Emma staring at the stage.

Two people were standing there now. A man with a loincloth like the waiter. His coffee-colored skin was oiled so that it gleamed, and a mask hid his face.

The young woman with him was wearing a ripped dress and also a mask. She stood with her arms above her head, chained to a vertical bar held in place by two upright posts. Her legs were spread about eighteen inches apart and chained to another crosspiece.

Lord, was that Karen Hopewell? Cole stared at her, trying to figure out if it was the woman they'd been sent to spring from this place. After several moments, he decided it wasn't her. The hair color was wrong, and she looked heavier than Karen.

Beside him, Emma tensed, and Cole reached down to take her hand.

On the stage, the man walked to the woman and began running his hands over her body. Then he gripped one of the tears in her dress and ripped at it, leaving a long gash in the fabric. He found another open place and pulled away more fabric, exposing more of her skin. Just as he shredded the dress enough to reach inside and caress her breasts, the lights went down again. When they came up, the couple on the stage was gone.

"Aw," Henry muttered. "It was just getting good."

"A little tease," Del Conte purred.

The main course came. Roast beef. Cole asked for rare and was able to choke some down. Again, the lights dimmed and came up to reveal a couple on stage. He was pretty sure the entertainment featured the same man and woman, only this time the guy was the one tied up.

The woman was cracking a whip when the lights flashed brightly, just before the room was plunged into darkness, and this time Cole was pretty sure it wasn't part of the performance.

A woman screamed, then went silent.

Next to Emma, their host pushed back his chair.

"What the hell is going on?" he asked in a hard voice.

CHAPTER NINE

Cole's sharp ears picked up scuffling sounds. He knew there were two or three were more people in the room than there had been, but he couldn't tell how many.

The darkness put him and Emma in danger, but it also provided them with an opportunity, if they didn't get killed in the process.

He reached for Emma's hand. Together they stood.

"What's happening?" Henry called out.

"Stay in your seats and stay calm," Del Conte answered.

Ignoring him, Cole led Emma around the side of the room toward the hidden door where their host had entered. She instantly understood what he was doing, helping him feel along the wall until they reached a seam.

"Here," she whispered.

He pushed at several locations, frustrated when the door wouldn't open.

Behind them in the dark, a shot rang out.

"Jesus!" Cole whispered. He'd thought that using the riot or whatever you called it was a good excuse to do some exploring, but if they didn't get out of here soon, they might not get out alive.

He felt Emma stumble sideways and knew she'd found the secret to opening the door from this side. They tumbled through into a dimly lit corridor, and Cole quickly closed the door behind them.

"What happened?" Emma asked.

"Don't know. But I'm hoping we're in a private part of the ship. And if anybody asks what we're doing here, we're escaping from the captain's ill-fated party."

"Right."

Running feet made them both stop short. Emma pulled Cole into a side passage just before armed guards came pounding down the hall.

As soon as they were alone again, they kept going. Cole was in the lead, and he gasped as water he hadn't seen hit him in the face.

"What the hell?"

Emma dodged to the side, avoiding the deluge. As he raised his head and blinked into the subdued light, he realized they had come out into a room with an artificial waterfall and a pool. The entrance to the tunnel was behind the cascading water, but he'd charged right through.

Cursing, he backed up, following Emma along a dry walkway.

He was soaking wet now, and mad as hell at himself for blundering into this space without looking where he was going. What if the tunnel had led to an animal cage?

All right, unlikely.

He and Emma moved to the side of the room, which was illuminated by emergency lighting. Screened by tropical greenery, they looked around.

Away from the cascading water, he could hear parrots cawing and people talking. Did he see the glint of metal bars on the other side of the open space? It was hard to tell. But he was sure he caught Karen Hopewell's scent.

Was she here?

They stopped to listen to the conversation at the bar.

"The lights went out for a minute. What happened?"

"Some kind of malfunction, I guess."

"We paid enough for this trip. They better get everything working again."

"Go over and intimidate the girl in the cage, if you want to have some fun. Just remember—no touching."

Cole strained to see who was talking and made out casually dressed men and women gathered around an open-sided thatched hut with a bar and stools on four sides. The men were wearing tropical shirts and shorts or slacks. The woman were in shorts and halter tops or shirts.

"Where's Del Conte?" somebody called out.

"Or Big Ben."

"Is this a hinky fantasy scenario?" someone asked.

Running footsteps came tramping through the underbrush, moving fast.

A woman screamed as a man dressed like a black-clad ninja launched himself at one of the guests, knocking him off the stool.

Chaos erupted, with people shouting and running in all directions.

"Stay here," Cole ordered Emma as he charged forward. He didn't know what was happening except that one of the guests had been attacked.

He leaped toward the men on the ground just as the one in black raised a hand with a knife.

Cole grabbed the arm, pulling it back, bringing a scream to the attacker's lips.

As he and the man grappled, he heard a scuffle in back of him. Another attacker materialized, and Emma leaped on him.

Christ, no.

Fear fueled his strength. Intent on immobilizing the ninja he was fighting, he yanked the man's arm back, hearing bone crack.

"Watch him," he shouted to the people who had been lounging around the bar as he scrambled up and turned toward the attacker Emma had taken on. But she already had him down. With a hand in his hair, she slammed his face against the floor, then lifted his head and did it again.

More men charged into the room, and Cole prepared for another attack.

"The next person who moves is dead," a hard voice said.

Cole went still, as did everyone else around him.

"What the hell is going on?" the voice asked.

"Ben, thank God," a woman said.

The newcomer nodded to her before turning to Cole. "You, Mason, what the hell are you doing here?"

It took a minute for Cole to realize the guy was talking to him, since he'd only acquired the name Mason a few hours earlier, strange as that seemed after so much had happened. He raised his head and saw the speaker was the man who had taken charge after the incident at the entry port.

Before he could answer, Emma had started talking, her voice sounding high and shaky, and he knew she wasn't faking her panic. "What are we doing here? I'd like to know! We were having dinner with Mr. Del Conte. Then the damn lights went off in the dining room and somebody started shooting. Cole and I were desperate to get out of there. We were fumbling along the wall, and a door opened, and we ran down a tunnel. It ended here. Then Cole walked into the waterfall and we were trying to figure out where we were— when these guys rushed in and started attacking everyone."

She stopped, dragged in a breath and huffed it out, giving a good imitation of a ditz brain who'd run out of steam.

"That's right," one of the men said. "We were attacked, and this man and woman were trying to help."

"We're Cole Mason and Emma Ray," he said.

"Get up," Ben ordered.

As Cole scrambled to his feet, guards rushed in and grabbed the men dressed in black and also Cole and Emma.

"Not them. They saved us when the other ones attacked," a woman protested.

"We'll sort it out," Ben said.

The guards kept hold of Cole and Emma, marching them across the room.

They passed the area where he'd spotted the glint of metal and saw bars. A cage. For one of the animals that was supposed to have escaped?

He looked more closely and saw a redheaded woman, standing with her shoulders against the far wall.

His heart clunked inside his chest when he smelled her scent very strongly. It was definitely Karen Hopewell.

As they approached, he tried to determine her condition. Her hair was coifed. Her face was made up, and she was wearing a white, see-through kimono and nothing else besides a butterfly clip in her hair. In the corner of the cell he spotted a bucket for her to use as a toilet.

For a second, their eyes met. She couldn't know who he was, but she seemed to be silently pleading with him to rescue her.

There was nothing he could say to her. She was alive, but she was on display in a way that obviously terrified her—and sickened him. He evaluated his chances of breaking free from four armed guards and knew he'd only get himself killed—and maybe Emma, too. They'd have to get back here later.

Still, the look on Karen's face made him want to leap to the bars and yank the door open. Only logic kept him from doing it.

He turned his head toward Emma and knew she had seen Karen as well. Like Cole, all she could do was walk past. Moments later, they exited the big party room and were herded down another hallway.

The guy named Ben stopped in front of a door and knocked.

"Come in," a voice called. It was Del Conte.

Two guards stayed on either side of Cole and Emma. Two more stood behind them with guns. Not good odds for an escape attempt, but if the conversation between Ben and Del Conte went the wrong way, they might have to risk it.

Cole's hearing was excellent, and he could pick up the exchange on the other side of the door.

"I have Cole Mason and Emma Ray."

"They disappeared from the dining room during the attack."

"They claim they were trying to escape the fracas and found your private door. They ended up in the Tropical Lounge."

"And then?"

"There was a knife attack."

"A knife attack! From whom?"

"Cast members."

"They shouldn't have been able to get in there. Or into the private dining room for that matter."

"Someone must have given them the code to the Tropical Lounge door. And they disabled the guard outside the dining room."

"How is that possible?"

"We're investigating."

"What about Mason and Ray? What was their role in this?"

"The guests said they came to their rescue."

"Do you believe that?"

"It sounds plausible, but both of them were on the offensive when I came in. They looked like trained fighters."

"I want you to focus on their background check. And on how security was breached."

"Meanwhile, what do we do with Mason and Ray?"

There was a pause. "Treat them like ordinary guests."

"Yes, sir."

"Send them in here. I want to hear their story."

"Yes sir."

The door opened again and Ben came out. "Mr. Del Conte would like to speak to you."

"Of course."

As Cole and Emma stepped through the door, Del Conte kept his gaze on them as he gestured toward the guest chairs across from his desk.

They sat.

Emma shot Cole a quick glance before clasping her hands in her lap. Probably she wanted to speak up the way she had previously, but hopefully she understood that this was between the men.

He looked around the plush office, taking in the artwork and the expensive furnishings.

"Is that a real Picasso?" he asked.

"Yes," Del Conte snapped as he inspected Cole's wet hair and clothing. "What happened to you?"

He grimaced. "I didn't know you had an indoor waterfall."

"You would have, if you'd taken the normal route to the Tropical Lounge."

"I didn't know you had a Tropical Lounge. It's not on the map."

"It's a restricted area for special guests."

"What's the normal route there?"

"An invitation from me."

"Well, when the shooting started in the dining room, we thought it might be prudent to leave."

"A reasonable decision. But how did you find my private doorway? That's not on the map, either."

"We saw you come in," Cole answered, "so we knew where it would be."

Del Conte nodded. "I should thank you for coming to the aid of my guests."

"No problem," Cole answered. "But perhaps you could tell us about the attacks. There was a disturbance when we arrived. Then in the dining room—and the Tropical Lounge."

"There's some unrest among my crew members."

"And they're trying to kill your paying guests?" Cole snapped.

"It seems some of the people my senior staff hired were not properly vetted. I'll have the situation back under control shortly."

"I hope so. I thought this was a safe place to bring my sweetie for some fun and games."

"It is!" Del Conte snapped. "In fact, I'd like to make amends by inviting you to the party I'm giving tomorrow morning for special invited guests only."

Cole felt his chest tighten. He wanted to refuse, but he knew this must be some kind of test. Del Conte had invited them to dinner. Now he wanted to observe them in a party situation. Presumably with people he trusted. He looked at Emma. "How about it, honey?"

"Sure," she said in a weak voice, and he knew her reaction was the same as his. But she understood the stakes.

"What kind of party?" he asked.

"We're using a Mayan theme."

"Uh huh."

"It's very appealing. You may find it as interesting as your love of Ancient Roman and Greek culture. It's at eleven on Deck Three. You should arrive an hour early—to give you time to get into costume."

"Costume?"

"Of course. That always enhances the reality of the fantasy experience."

He stared at them for several seconds then turned back to the papers on his desk.

Stinger Henderson pushed his chair away from the computer, stood and brushed back his long hair. He'd been hunched over the keyboard for hours, and he stretched cramped muscles before striding down the hall to Frank Decorah's office and knocking.

"Come in," his boss called.

Decorah, who had come straight back after dropping off Cole and Emma in Florida, looked up, his eyes bloodshot and wary. He'd given orders not to be disturbed unless absolutely necessary. And he'd put other assignments aside to personally focus on the Karen Hopewell kidnapping. He'd given orders not to be disturbed unless absolutely necessary.

Seeing the worried look on his computer guy's face, he snapped, "What's the bad news now?"

"I've been monitoring the online information pertaining to Cole Mason's legend."

"It's not holding up?"

"It's holding so far. But someone is doing a lot of checking into the details. Not just his. Also Emma's."

"Someone from Del Conte's security, I take it."

"That's a good assumption."

"Make sure they get the right impression."

"I'm trying. But there may be ways to get around the story we've built up."

"Perfect," Decorah muttered. "Are you telling me Cole and Emma are in more danger than we anticipated?"

"Yes."

"We can't pull them out. I mean even if we wanted to, there's no way to reach them." He gave Stinger a direct look. "Do what you can to protect their cover."

"I am. I just want you to be prepared in case we have to come up with some other way to spring the Hopewell woman."

"We've got a ship standing by, but it's not equipped to attack the *Windward*. And if it did, that might trigger undesirable actions on Del Conte's part."

"Like killing the hostage—and Cole and Emma, too."

"Exactly."

Cole exited Del Conte's office.

Glancing back, he saw Emma following him, her gait stiff. His emotions were churning. He wanted to take her back to their room, lock the door and pull her into his arms so that he could comfort her—and himself.

He made a dismissive sound. Not exactly the right strategy for two operatives on a mission.

Which meant he had to jerk himself out of defensive mode. About fifty feet down the hall he slowed his pace and allowed her to catch up with him.

"That was annoying." he said aloud. "I don't like being attacked when I'm on vacation—then dressed down by the cruise director."

"Try to relax," Emma answered, unwittingly helping to set up the scenario he'd decided on. He leaned toward her, speaking in a barely audible voice. "I think this might be a good time for us to have a fight."

"What?"

"Be on the outs."

He raised his voice again. "I spent a lot of cash on this vacation, but I'm not having much fun. And you're part of the problem."

"You're blaming what just happened on me?"

"You weren't exactly being friendly to Del Conte."

"You just said you didn't like the way he was treating us."

"But he did invite us to something interesting tomorrow."

"You know I don't want to do it," Emma retorted, speaking for the character she was playing and for herself as well.

"Well, you damn well better."

She gave him a stormy look as they stepped into the elevator, probably wondering what he had in mind, exactly.

When they reached Deck Seven, he stepped out and marched down the hall, keeping several paces ahead of her, thinking about what he was going to do next.

Once they were in their room, he turned to face her with an annoyed expression on his face. "I'm getting tired of your acting like a wet blanket."

"And I'm getting tired of your crazy suggestions. Like having your mark tattooed on me. Or playing that I'm a witch. You think that would be fun for me?"

"The witch stuff was Del Conte's idea, but I can see it. If you get into the spirit of the experience."

"Oh please. After you had me shaved, what would you do, whip me?"

"Yes. You're being a pain in the ass."

"I'm being . . . sensible."

"Well, if you don't like what the ship has to offer, you can sulk in the room. I'm going out to have some fun."

"What?" she wheezed, and he could see she was genuinely startled.

"You can stay here and play with yourself, if that's all you can think of to do."

She swallowed hard. "Cole, please."

"We'll talk about it later."

"When will you be back?"

"I don't know. Don't wait up for me."

She stared at him. "You're still wet from that waterfall."

He stopped short and looked down at his clothing. "Damn."

Muttering under his breath, he whirled toward the closet and took out a clean shirt and pants. She watched him throw his ruined clothes on the floor, then change into a new set. He strode toward the door, then stopped and turned.

"Lock the door behind me."

"What?"

"Lock the door, and stay in here."

"And if I want to enjoy this place on my own?"

"I wouldn't recommend it."

Bruno Del Conte stood up and walked to the liquor cabinet at the far end of his office and poured himself a single malt Scotch. After downing it in one gulp, he poured another shot and sat back down at his desk, this time sipping from the glass.

Things were getting out of control in a way that astonished him. The fat guy from the dinner party had been shot in the arm and was recovering in the infirmary. Thank God nobody else had been injured. The perpetrators were being interrogated now, but so far they hadn't implicated anyone else.

But how had they gotten into the private rooms?

He fought a sick feeling that he hadn't experienced in years. Long ago when he'd watched his father with Dieter, he'd known that he should be the one enjoying that warm, close relationship. Fate—and a drunken accident—had changed everything, and Bruno had vowed never to be in a position of weakness again.

He wasn't going to slip into that hell on earth again.

Turning to the computer, he sent out an executive order.

"All slaves not currently entertaining guests will be placed in lockdown. All requests for private entertainment will be cleared through security. Security will be increased in all public areas with staff working double shifts if necessary."

Then he fired off a memo to Ben. "Interrogate the man and woman who were entertaining at the dinner. Find out if they let the attackers in."

His own honor and satisfaction demanded that he keep the upper hand.

He reached for the phone and called Greg, one of his trusted security men.

"Yes sir?"

"Have Karen Hopewell moved from the Tropical Lounge to the brig on Deck Three. Immediately."

"Yes sir."

Issuing the orders made him feel better. He would not lose control over his own ship. He'd blow the damn thing up before he let that happen.

Which was an option. He could escape in the boat he kept at the ready. Then activate the charges that were already in place.

It would be sad to lose the ship, but it was insured.

And he could figure out how to start again—more safely.

The decision made him feel better.

Emma stared at the closed door, trying to understand what Cole was doing. When they'd left Del Conte's office, all she had wanted to do was get back here and reach for him.

Instead, he'd just walked out. Leaving her confused, angry and feeling hollow inside.

She'd thought she was starting to understand him. Apparently not. She had half a mind to follow him down the corridor, screaming at him. Would Emma Ray do that, or would she roll over and do what her sugar daddy ordered?

Still unsure of her ultimate decision, she crossed the room on shaky legs and locked the door, hardly able to believe how fast everything had changed.

Cole had started a fight—and used that as an excuse to leave her in the room. What the hell was he thinking? Had he decided he could explore better on his own? Or what?

She sighed, aware that she'd gotten emotionally involved in the scenario they'd been acting out for the benefit of the people who were bugging this room. But her nerves were already raw, and she couldn't hold her reactions in check.

She paced from the door to the bathroom and back again. It would serve him right if she went out and did some investigating on her own.

As soon as that plan formed, a chill went through her. This was a dangerous environment for a woman alone. Some guy would hit on her, and she'd have to fend him off. Maybe with extreme prejudice. Which would be out of character for Emma Ray.

But Cole wouldn't have any problems with the female staff and guests. And apparently he'd had something in mind when he'd left.

Better wait for him to report back.

Still, his strategy galled her. Not just the strategy. His failure to consult her before leaving. Another male who assumed she'd just fall in line with what he wanted.

The thought sent her mind spinning in another direction. Back to the conversation in the car when she'd taken offense at his talking about her family. But if she was honest, she'd admit that she'd joined Decorah Security to get away from the domination of her father, who'd run their household like a military base. Either you obeyed the rules, or you were punished, often with his belt.

Still, she'd hung on his tales of outwitting thugs, white collar criminals and government operatives. Even so, there was no way she'd work for Kent Richards. Then she'd taken a class with Frank Decorah and thought that maybe he was the right kind of boss, even when she'd been prepared to leave if it turned out she'd made the wrong judgment call.

The job had worked out. Better than she'd hoped. She'd built a career in the company. But was Cole Marshall going to screw that up?

Not necessarily, she told herself. This is just one evening during one assignment. And she wasn't going to throw their personal relationship into the mix.

She took a deep breath and then another, struggling to calm herself. Getting mad at Cole wasn't going to do either one of them any good. And how *was he* supposed to consult her? They were in an environment where the walls had ears, to use an old cliché. Maybe even eyes.

Too bad she didn't know Morse code. Then they could have had a constructive conversation before he left. Unless he really was angry with her.

She stopped herself again. That made no sense. It was Cole Mason who was mad. Not Cole Marshall. She hoped.

A number of women in the bars around the *Windward* received some new information. One of them was Stella Marie who was often assigned to the entertainment areas. Although she was dressed like an elegant companion, she was on the security staff. When the transmitter in her right ear buzzed, she went still as she listened to a hard voice giving instructions. She'd been working in the Royal Island Lounge this evening, keeping an eye on the guests at the gaming tables. Now she hurried to the door and scanned the corridor, looking for a tall man with dark hair and dark eyes who might be coming her way. He'd had a fight with his girlfriend, and she was supposed to ease his pain.

Cole got off the elevator on Deck Three, not quite sure where he was going. He'd had no concrete plans. He'd only known that he and Emma's emotions were too raw for them to remain in the same room.

Or—to put it another way—if they stayed in the same room together, they'd end up making love again to relieve their tension, and he was determined not to let that happen.

He sighed. He'd never gotten his business and personal life more mixed up. Which was another reason why he'd decided to go off alone. He might not find Karen, but at least he knew Emma was safe for the next few hours.

So now what?

He'd been talking with one of the entertainment consultants when he'd gotten the message about Del Conte inviting them to dinner. There had been no problem about locating him on the ship, which meant that he'd probably been under observation all along.

He'd stormed out of the room saying that he was going to have a good time. He thought about the Tropical Lounge where Karen was being held. Del Conte had said you needed special status to get invited there. But maybe he could wangle an invite. What if he made friends with one of the guests who could get in there.

"You alone?"

A woman spoke nearby, and he looked up to see a slender brunette wearing a clingy, low-cut emerald green evening gown. She was standing at the entrance to a lounge area. Inside he could see comfortable couches and hear low, sultry music.

"I am."

Tall and elegant, she looked at him as though he was the most fascinating man in the world. An interesting technique. Another time he might have walked on past, but she was providing him with an opportunity he shouldn't turn down.

A smile flickered on her lips. "You're Cole Mason."

He tipped his head to the side, staring at her. "How do you know?"

"The staff has a list of guests."

"I guess that makes sense," he answered, wondering how many people had been watching for him.

She studied him with interest. "Didn't you come to the *Windward* with your girlfriend?"

"Yes. But she's . . ." He paused, wondering how to put it. "She's not into this place."

"Too bad. But that doesn't mean you can't have some fun."

"I was thinking the same thing."

"Come sit down." She led him into the dimly lit room with comfortable couches scattered about, much like the setup on the hovercraft when they'd come over from Miami.

They wove their way to a far corner where he stood for a moment beside a plush couch—until she took his hand and eased him down.

"Why don't we get comfortable."

He sat, wondering if she could get him into that Tropical Lounge—if he asked nicely.

Almost immediately, a hostess wearing a bikini glided over. She and the woman in the green dress exchanged a quick glance. "What can I get you to drink?"

"Soda water with lime," Cole answered.

The server raised an eyebrow. "Nothing stronger?"

"I prefer keeping my wits about me."

"A sound plan. Too bad more of our guests don't follow it."

The hostess withdrew, leaving him alone with his new friend.

"My name's Stella," she said, sliding along the couch so that her thigh was pressed to his.

"Cole, as you already know."

"Uh huh. But I don't know what you like to do when you let your hair down."

"Well, that Tropical Lounge I saw looked pretty nifty. Can I get in there?"

"I think it can be arranged."

"No bull?"

She smiled. "If that's what you want. No bull."

She laid her hand on his thigh, stroking. He felt nothing. He'd bonded with Emma, and he wasn't interested in any other woman. When her hand crept inward toward his crotch, he lifted it away.

"Don't."

"You don't want to play with me?"

"I want to play, but with my girlfriend."

"She's not available."

"I'll wait till she is," he answered, then said, "You're good at your job. How did you get here?"

"I heard about the ship and signed a one-year contract."

"You like it?"

Something he couldn't read flickered across her face. "Yes."

"You take part in . . . scenes?"

"Yes."

"What are you trained to do?"

105

"I can be either a dominant or a submissive."

"Which do you like better?"

"I like them both—when I get into the spirit of the thing."

"What if you're not in the mood?"

"The pay's good enough to put me in the mood."

The hostess set the drinks on the low table in front of them, and Cole took a swallow. To his werewolf senses, it tasted strange, and he set the glass down again.

"I hear some of the scenes get a little rough. Does anyone get hurt?"

"We have strict rules about how far we can go."

Yeah, he thought. I'll bet.

The woman took a sip of her drink. He left his on the table. It had an unpleasant quality, and he thought he shouldn't have any more.

He should steer the conversation back to the previous topic. "In that Tropical Lounge, I saw a girl in a cage. Could a guy get in there with her, and you know . . ."

"I thought you only wanted to play with your girlfriend."

"She could come too." He laughed at his clever joke, then leaned back, feeling a little dizzy. Damn, what the hell was wrong with him?

When he looked at the drink sitting on the table, insight struck. It had been drugged, and it hadn't taken much of what was in the soda water to make a werewolf woozy.

With a low curse, he started to push himself up. "I'd better go."

Her eyes had a satisfied gleam. "You look like you're not feeling well. I'll help you."

"No," he protested, hardly able to get the word out.

"I think you need to lie down."

In his blurry vision, he saw Stella make a motion with her hand. Moments later, a burly man appeared at Cole's side. "Leave me alone," he muttered.

Some of the other people in the room turned toward him, then quickly looked away. Obviously they didn't want to get involved.

"Take me back to my room," he said, hearing the slurred quality of the words.

"I'm afraid you're not going to make it," Stella said in a firm voice. She and the guy led him out a back door and down the hall. He tried to pull away, but he didn't have the ability to make his muscles work well enough.

How far was it to the room? A thousand miles.

"Emma," he called out, his voice still slurred. She didn't answer because she wasn't there, and he knew he never should have walked out on her tonight. If he'd stayed and made love to her, he wouldn't be in trouble now.

His head was pounding, making it hard to think as the woman and the man led him down the corridor to another room. He couldn't see the number on the door, but inside was another suite. They led him across a sitting area and dumped him on the bed. When he tried to get up, the woman pressed a hand to his shoulder. She was surprisingly strong. Or he was weak as a puppy.

"Got to go," he muttered, feeling his heart thumping inside his chest.

"After you answer some questions."

The woman picked up the phone beside the bed, dialed a number and spoke. Although Cole couldn't hear what she was saying, he felt her hand caressing his face, felt her fingers drift down his body and press over his cock, rocking against him, but he didn't respond.

"What's wrong with you? You're limp as a slug. I thought you came here to have a good time," she murmured.

"With Emma," he answered.

"Then why were you asking about the girl in the cage?"

A trick question.

"Curiosity," he muttered.

"Oh come on."

"Leave me alone." He closed his eyes, needing to sleep.

"The girl in the cage excites you, but I don't?

"Emma excites me."

"I'll get her."

Through slitted eyes, he saw the woman stand up. He should leave and find Emma, only he didn't think he could get to his feet.

He lay with his eyes closed, drifting again. Someone sat down beside him. "Honey, I'm glad I found you."

"Emma?" he asked. It sounded like her. "You smell wrong," he muttered.

"A new perfume."

"I don't like perfume."

"I'll wash it off before we go to bed."

He tried to open his eyes, but she pressed one hand over his closed lids while she slid the other down his body, stroking his nipples through his shirt, making them stiffen before gliding downward, pressing over his cock.

"Emma?"

"Mumm," she answered as she began to caress him through his slacks, arousing him.

"That's better."

She unbuckled his belt, then opened the button at the top of his slacks before lowering the zipper and reaching inside, pulling his penis out.

"Nice equipment," she murmured as she clasped her fist around him, stroking up and down with a teasing pressure that had his hips rising in response. When she stopped, he made a pleading sound.

After a moment, she replaced her hand with her mouth, taking him into the warm, wet cavity and sucking strongly for a moment before lifting her face away and blowing on him.

He moaned. "Don't stop."

"You like me to make you come this way? Is it better than fucking?"

He'd never done that with Emma. His eyes flew open to find the woman in the green dress grinning down at him.

When he tried to wrench away, she held him fast. "So you *can* get it up," she purred.

Another voice intruded. "What the hell are you doing?"

"Having some fun with a guy who probably doesn't like to be submissive," a woman's voice answered. Definitely not Emma.

"You're not here to screw around. Put his johnson back in his pants."

He felt his penis being shoved back into his trousers.

A large hand shook his shoulder. "Let's get back to business."

CHAPTER TEN

Cole's eyes blinked open, and he found himself staring at the hard-jawed guy named Ben. From security. Big Ben, the people in the Tropical Lounge had called him.

"Where's Emma?" Cole asked. Jesus, had this guy been watching them?

"She's not here. I'm asking the questions. What are you doing on the *Windward*?"

Cole thought about that carefully. He was here on assignment—to rescue Karen Hopewell, but he'd better not talk about that.

"Came to have a good time." he managed to answer.

"Who are you working for?"

Cole fought confusion, struggling to remember the answers that were in the dossier he'd read. "Have my own company."

"Doing what?"

"Uh . . . car detailing."

"Un huh. What's your name?"

Another trick question. He had a real name, but he wasn't using on the *Windward*. "Cole Mason," he finally answered.

The guy took Cole's chin in his hand. "Your real name. Hurry up."

"Cole Mason," he repeated, hanging on to coherence by his fingernails, wondering if that was the right answer.

It didn't sound quite right. Maybe he should give his other name.

No. That was the wrong thing to do. On this ship, he was Cole Mason.

The man straightened and spoke to the woman. "How much did he drink?"

"A big swallow."

"Maybe that's not enough to make him tell the truth. But I'll give it another try."

If someone had told Emma a week ago that she'd be all wound up with Cole Marshall, she would have called him a liar. That was then. This was now.

Struggling to keep from cursing aloud, she paced back and forth across the carpet in the luxury suite, her hands clenched into fists as she tried to contain her roiling emotions.

Where the hell was that bastard who was supposed to be her partner on this assignment? He'd left hours ago, and she had no idea where he had gone. Was he out there on Bruno Del Conte's pleasure craft having the time of his life? Or had he gotten himself into trouble? And now he needed her. Only she had no idea where to even start looking for him.

That thought made her chest clench. She was worried about him with an all-consuming anxiety that threatened to drive her insane.

It was almost impossible to keep herself from charging out of the room and start searching for him. But her rational self knew that was a very bad idea.

Which meant she was reduced to silent cursing. And brooding.

"Damn you," she muttered aloud, wondering if somebody was watching her or listening. And laughing their ass off because she was just another bimbo who'd been brought here by a boyfriend who found the ship's delights more tempting than his old familiar partner.

But what if he needed her? Again her stomach clenched. Too bad he wasn't wearing a transponder so she could track him. But there hadn't been time for that kind of advanced preparation.

Cole lay on the bed, listening to the conversation around him. He was sure the people talking were standing right there beside him, but their voices seemed to be coming to him from far away.

"I'm talking to you, loser. Pay attention. Who did you come here with?"

He struggled to wrap his mouth around the answer.

"Emma."

"Emma who?"

"Emma . . . Ray." He thought about it for a moment. "That's a weird name, don't you think?" he muttered, then wondered why he'd volunteered the information

"Did she have another name before you brought her to the *Windward*?"

"Huh?"

"Is that her real name."

"Unless she lied to me," he answered. He laughed at his own witticism.

"What's your business on the *Windward*," the guy said. Had he asked that question before? How many questions had he asked? Were they going over everything again? Cole couldn't be sure.

"Your business on the *Windward*," the guy prompted.

"Did you ask me that before?"

"Yeah. Answer me."

"Not business, pleasure," he muttered, struggling to hold it together. He closed his eyes, drifting. Did he hear another question? Or was that just something echoing in his head?

The man named Ben shook him hard, his voice insistent, but Cole did his best to ignore the distraction. He was done with answering.

"You'd better be straight with me," the man said. It sounded like he was shouting in Cole's ear.

"Let me sleep," he muttered.

"I don't think we're going to get anything more out of him," the interrogator said. "Not right now. Maybe with something stronger. Go get the . . ."

He didn't hear what it was.

"I need authorization," the woman answered. "That stuff can really mess with his mind."

"I'm giving you authorization," Ben snapped. "If Mickey has any objections, tell him to call me."

Cole had stopped paying attention to the conversation, but he sensed the woman walking away from the bed. When the door closed behind her, Cole hoped they'd leave him alone for a while.

Instead Ben gripped his shoulder and shook him hard.

"Cut it out."

"Let's try again, while she's gone."

"No."

"You don't get a choice. I said, we're trying again."

"Let me sleep."

In a surprising move, the guy slapped him hard across the face. The ringing blow stung. Cole blinked, his mind swimming back to some semblance of coherence.

"What the hell?'

"Did I get your attention, buddy?" the man said in a harsh voice.

Cole tensed.

When the guy pulled back his hand again, Cole rolled away and came up swinging.

Putting everything he could into the blow, he connected with Ben's jaw, and the man fell back, sprawling on the floor.

113

Cole stared at him, trying to make his mind work. "Got to get out of here," he muttered as he pushed himself off the bed and staggered toward the door.

He didn't entirely understand what was happening, but he knew that he had to get away before the woman came back—and they gave him something that was going to make him feel worse.

Somehow he stayed on his feet and staggered toward the door.

It seemed impossibly far away, but finally he made it across the carpet, then into the corridor where he stood swaying. He didn't have much time. The woman might come back at any minute, and he'd better not be here when she did.

Cole steadied himself with a hand against the wall, struggling to clear his head as he inched along. He was in danger of falling on his face with every step, but he was also desperate to get out of the hallway.

"Oh Christ," he muttered as he kept stumbling along.

Did he hear footsteps? Was the woman coming back? With the drug that was going to mess with his brain even more. He couldn't let her catch him.

Gritting his teeth, he picked up his pace and made it to the next door. Praying that it was unlocked, he twisted the knob. At least he'd been granted a bit of luck. The door opened, and he tumbled inside, closing the barrier behind him. He flopped to the carpet, breathing hard, struggling not to pass out. But the exertion had wiped out the last of his strength, and he lost the battle for consciousness.

Stella stepped back into the interrogation room, looking around in confusion. "What the hell happened? Where is he?"

From where he sat on the rug with his back pressed against the side of the bed, Ben looked up into Stella's incredulous face.

He made an angry sound. "The bastard decked me and got away."

"How could he deck you? He was in pretty bad shape."

"I made a mistake and got rough with him. I guess it woke him up enough to fight me off."

"And he knocked you out?"

"Don't rub it in."

She kept her gaze fixed on him. "We were supposed to get the real dope on his background. I'd like to be there when you explain to Del Conte how you screwed up."

Ben scowled at her. "It's my problem, not yours. I'll take care of it." He cleared his throat. "But you were here during the interrogation. He gave all the right answers. Lying would be impossible after drinking that stuff."

"Then why did you want to give him something stronger?"

"As a precaution." He sighed. "This would have been a quick fix. But I'll keep digging into his background. And Emma Ray's. Maybe that's the only way to break his story."

"Are we going to look for him?"

"For now, let's leave him on the loose and see where he turns up. If he's gone to ground somewhere, we can start searching."

"Can he make it back to his room, do you think?"

"Maybe. If he does, we should find out something when his honey starts asking questions about where he's been. Too bad we didn't douse him with perfume so she could get really mad."

Stella laughed. "Before he drank the stuff, he seemed uptight."

"Maybe the drug loosened him up. Maybe he'll say something he wouldn't otherwise."

Cole's eyes snapped open. For long moments he lay very still, dragging in gulps of air and letting them trickle from his lungs as he struggled to figure out why he was lying on the carpet of a room he didn't remember entering.

Easy, he told himself. *Take it easy. What's the last thing you remember?*

Walking down a corridor.

And then?

Nothing.

The absolute void sent a wave of panic surging through him.

He moaned and moved his paw against the carpet.

His paw?

Looking down at his body, he saw gray fur.

Jesus. Somewhere along the line he'd changed to wolf form.

Fighting rising panic, he forced himself to lie very still and catalogue sensations. The soft fibers of the rug under his furry body. The throbbing of powerful engines. The pounding in his head.

There were only two reasons why he would have changed. Because he was in danger. Or for the pleasure of running through the forest.

One thing he knew, there were no forests here. He might not remember the past few . . . hours? But he knew he was on a ship.

The name of the craft came to him. It was the *Windward*. He remembered coming here. With Emma.

Oh Lord, where was Emma?

He wanted to howl, only someone would hear him if he did.

Instead, he tried to bring his recent life into focus; but the memories swimming in his mind were blurry. Had Big Ben been asking him questions? Had he met a woman?

He had a vague recollection of someone with dark hair and a green dress. Was he making that up? If not, what had he done with her?

His throat clenched as he fought to maintain his sanity. Something had happened. Something bad.

In the dim light filtering in through the window, he looked around. He saw a wide bed, a dresser. A door that probably led to a bathroom.

The accommodations were upscale, but not quite as luxurious as the suite he and Emma had been assigned.

As he thought of her, his throat clenched again. They'd been fighting.

Why?

So he could leave the room, he thought, but he wasn't sure.

But he should never have abandoned her. He started for the door, then remembered he couldn't turn the damn knob with his paw. Or walk the corridors of the ship, for that matter. When they'd first arrived and heard gunshots, they'd been told that an animal had escaped.

Were there really animals here? And even if the explanation was a lie, a lone wolf was going to attract attention.

Yeah, right.

He forced himself to stand on legs that weren't quite steady. His mouth was dry as cotton and tasted awful. He needed a drink, but he couldn't get one until he changed.

Quickly he began to say the chant that changed him from wolf to man. Of course he couldn't speak it aloud as a wolf. But the familiar words surged through his head.

Taranis, Epona, Cerridwen, he recited, then repeated the same phrase and went on to another.

Soon his body would begin to change, the fur transmuting to skin. Muscles and tendons transforming from those of a wolf to a man.

Ga. Feart. . .

The sound of a doorknob turning had him stopping in mid-sentence.

Someone was coming into the room.

He hadn't gotten halfway through the chant, and he was still a wolf. Could he hide? Crawl behind the bed?

No. A wolf didn't hide. A wolf stood his ground.

A man stepped into the room and flipped on the light. A man wearing the uniform of Del Conte's security force.

He and the wolf both blinked in the sudden brightness.

"What the hell?"

There was a moment of astonishment when the man stared at the savage beast. Then his training kicked in, and a gun materialized in his hand.

CHAPTER ELEVEN

Before the man could get the gun into firing position, the wolf leaped on him, knocking him to the floor.

He might have gone for the gun hand, but then what? He didn't even have to think. He acted on instinct, his sharp teeth slashing through the flesh and bone of the man's neck.

He made a gurgling noise, struggling to fire his weapon. But it was already too late. The wolf's teeth slashed through the carotid artery.

Blood spurted, and the wolf sucked it in, caught in the exhilaration of the battle. It was over quickly.

As the man went still, the wolf stepped back, staring down at his prey.

But the wolf's thoughts fought the human insights in Cole's mind. He had killed. In self defense. Still, he had to deal with the consequences.

The fight had been brief, but it had weakened him. He dropped to the rug, panting, gathering his strength.

When he felt a little better, he staggered across the room and looked out, staying well back.

Mercifully, nobody was in the hall. What if a guest had been out there? Would he have had to kill him too?

He thrust that thought from his mind as he pushed the door closed with his head, waiting a minute while he gathered his resources again.

Then he began the chant that had been interrupted, feeling his muscles and tendons jerk, tasting blood in his mouth as he transformed into a naked man. Sucking air into his lungs, he staggered across the carpet toward the door and turned the lock.

Again he had to rest. This time he stared at the dead man on the floor, thinking about where to hide the body.

When the answer came to him, he laughed.

He was on a ship. All he had to do was toss the evidence overboard. Yeah, if he could get the body to an open deck without being questioned.

His brain was still fuzzy, and he struggled to plot out a plan of action. Finally, he decided that his best chance was in the guard's uniform. Too bad the shirtfront was soaked with blood. But the good news was that the blue color would hide some of the mess.

He stripped off the guy's shirt and pants, then took the shirt into the bathroom. First, he took a long drink of cold water. It helped to clear his head a little, which only made his lack of recent memories more disturbing. As he searched his mind for facts, he washed out as much of the blood from the shirt as he could.

The hair dryer at the sink came in handy for partially drying the fabric.

He dressed in the uniform, thankful that the clothing fit him reasonably well. His own clothes were in a heap on the floor where he must have torn them off. He folded them up so he could carry them over his arm.

Remembering the specifications of his own room, he went to the closet where he found the spare blanket neatly wrapped in a large plastic case.

Since rigor mortis hadn't yet set in, he was able to fold the body up and stuff it into the bag.

After making sure that the safety was off, he slid the gun into his pocket, hoping he didn't have to use it.

There was still a large bloodstain in the middle of the carpet, but that was going to be someone else's problem.

He stripped the spread off the bed, and folded it around the plastic case. Then he sat down heavily at the desk, resting again as he pulled out the *Windward* guest literature and determined the closest open deck and the best way to get there. He thought he was on Deck Three. He'd have to verify that. If so, he could get to the outside on Deck Four.

He was exhausted beyond belief, and it was tempting to simply leave the body in the room, but it would start to smell, security would come to investigate, and they'd find the man had been mauled by a large animal. Better to follow his original plan.

After taking several deep breaths, he got up and wiped off anything he might have touched before unlocking the door. Seeing the corridor was empty, he picked up the wrapped-up body and started down the hall, keeping his head down.

He made it to the stairwell without incident, and saw from the number on the door that Deck Four was the next one up.

Grimly he started to climb. But he'd made it only halfway when he heard voices above him.

He couldn't run back. His only option was to stop where he was and hope for the best.

Leaning against the wall, he put down the wrapped body and got out the gun, hoping he wasn't going to have to use it.

A young man and a woman came into view. He was blond and muscular. She was slender and Asian, and groaning softly as the man spoke quietly to her, supporting her weight. Naked to the waist, she looked like she'd been whipped.

As the man spotted a guard holding a gun, surprise and anger clouded his face. "What are you going to do, shoot us and claim we're part of the mutiny?"

"No."

The man snorted.

"Don't do anything foolish," Cole advised.

"What do we have to lose?"

"Everything. Just go on past. I'm not going to stop you."

"Why should we trust you?"

"Because I'm on your side."

The man answered with a harsh laugh.

The woman dug her fingers into his arm. "Come on," she whispered.

To his relief, they slipped quickly past him. Feeling queasy, he waited until they were a level down before picking up his bundle and heading up the stairs again. To his vast relief, he saw no one else.

On Deck Four, he stepped out of the stairwell and headed for the exterior of the ship.

He crossed quickly to the railing, hoisted the body up, and threw it over the side, hearing it splash as it hit the water and seeing the wrapping spread out in the water.

He hadn't weighted down the package because he'd known he couldn't carry anything extra. Maybe that wouldn't matter, since the *Windward* was moving at a good clip. Maybe sharks would take care of the evidence.

It was tempting to keep the guard's weapon, but having the gun in his possession was too incriminating. After a moment's hesitation, he tossed the gun over the side as well.

Again, he heard footsteps and faded into the shadows. This time it was an older man and a young woman, laughing and talking, obviously drunk. Hopefully, they wouldn't remember a random guard out on the deck.

When they had passed, he ducked into a storage closet and stood leaning against the wall. Had he really gotten away with murder?

Not murder. Self-defense he reminded himself.

Yeah, but the guard had only been doing his job.

On this hellhole of a ship.

Those thoughts chased themselves around in Cole's mind as he pulled off the uniform and put on his own clothes. After emerging from the closet, he tossed the uniform over the rail.

Now what?

Was it better to go back to the cabin?

Or leave Emma hanging out to dry on her own?

No choice at all, really. But where was his room, exactly. Deck Three?

No, they'd been moved to Deck Seven. Somehow he managed to dredge up the room number.

Almost too exhausted to stand, he headed for the stairs again. Centuries later, he finally located his room.

He couldn't find his key, and when he knocked on the door, nothing happened.

He knocked again, louder.

The door flew open, and Emma stepped into his line of vision.

A whole wealth of confused emotions welled inside him. Relief. Apology. Shame.

What he saw in her eyes was anger—which had to be fueled by worry.

"Where in the hell have you been?"

He hadn't been sure how he was going to act when he came in. Now he understood that he had to be Cole Mason.

As he shoved past her into the room, her voice followed him.

"I've been worried sick."

She stopped as she took a good look at him, and he could only imagine what she was seeing, if he looked as bad as he felt.

"Cole?"

"Be right back." He staggered across the room, made it to the bathroom, where he threw up the water he'd drunk. He stayed kneeling in front of the toilet longer than he needed to because he wasn't viewing his immediate future with happy anticipation.

After flushing the mess away, he grabbed a glass, filled it and cautiously rinsed out his mouth before taking a few cautious sips. He felt like hell and when he raised his face to look in the mirror, he was shocked by his appearance.

His face was pale. His skin sweaty. His hair mussed. If he'd seen this man on the street, he'd think he was recovering from a bender. Which was impossible in this case. A werewolf couldn't drink enough to get wasted.

That couldn't be what had precipitated this whole mess. But what?

Behind him, Emma appeared in the doorway. Her expression had changed from anger to worry. "What happened?"

He knew part of it. The part he couldn't tell her. And the rest of it was locked somewhere inside his churning brain.

Karen sat hunched over on the bunk in the cell where she'd been moved, wondering if she was ever going to get off the *Windward*. And wondering if she'd view the world the same way when and if she did.

As dark thoughts filled her mind, she shuddered and clasped her arms around her shoulders. She had dozed off when she sensed someone outside her cell.

Fearing she'd see another burly guard—or Del Conte, she looked up and found herself staring at a tall brunette woman wearing a green cocktail dress.

The woman gave her a sympathetic look. "How are you doing?"

Was it a trick question? What should she answer?

Finally, she shrugged.

"I'm sure this must be hard for you."

"Yes." She admitted, struggling to keep her voice from trembling.

"It would be good if you could give me some help."

"Like what?"

"Nothing difficult."

"Who are you?"

"Stella. A woman who works on the ship."

Karen tipped her head to the side. "What do you do?"

"I entertain guests."

Karen nodded, thinking that was probably a sucky job, no matter how polished and confident this woman looked.

She was carrying a large envelope. From it she pulled a couple of photographs, which she turned toward Karen.

"Do you know this man and woman?" she said.

Karen studied the picture. The man was dark-haired and tough looking. The woman was a pretty blond with short hair.

"Am I supposed to know them?"

This time it was Stella who shrugged.

Karen kept her gaze fixed on the pictures. If she said she knew these people, would it help her get out? And if she said she knew them, then what? As she stared at the pictures, she had a flash of memory.

"I think I saw them," she murmured.

The woman's shoulders straightened. "Where?"

"I think they came running through that room with the waterfall where I was at first."

"Yes, they did come through there. But you hadn't seen them before that?"

"No."

"Think carefully. You're sure?"

"Yes," she whispered, wishing she could be more helpful.

The woman's voice hardened. "You will be punished if you are lying."

Fear twisted Karen's stomach. "I'm not lying. I mean maybe she looks like somebody who was in my school."

Stella gave her a sharp look. "Your school?"

Karen shrugged. "I mean, I guess she wouldn't be here."

"What was her name?"

"Emma something. I don't remember."

The woman gave her a sharp look. "But it was Emma?"

"I'm not absolutely sure. I mean, it probably wasn't her."

"What school?"

"The Carlton Academy."

The woman spun on her heel and marched away, leaving Karen sick and shaking. Had she done the right thing? Or not?

On this ship of horrors, how could you know?

"What happened to you?"

The question sent a wave of panic surging through Cole. When he looked away from Emma, she grabbed his arm.

He dragged in a breath and let it out. He couldn't tell her the part with the guard and the wolf. Not now, because that would be a death sentence for both of them.

The rest of it was a blank. He'd pushed the bout of amnesia out of his mind during the crisis with the guard. Now it was back in the center of his mind.

He watched Emma's expression harden as she took in his reluctance to come clean with her. "You mean you won't tell me."

Anger and fear tangled on his face.

Punching out the words, he said, "I mean I don't know!" At least that was partly true.

He crossed the room, dropped onto the bed and lay down with his shoes on the spread, his arm over his face and his eyes closed. To his chagrin, he suddenly started to tremble, and he couldn't stop.

Emma's chest tightened. She had been so angry she'd been ready to slug Cole. Now she could see that something had shaken him to his core. Had he gotten dragged into some S and M scene that he couldn't handle? She didn't know, but all she wanted to do was help him. When she crossed the room and eased down beside him, he tensed.

"Leave me alone."

She reached to cup her hand around his shoulder. Keeping her tone gentle, she said, "This is a . . . seductive place. Did you do something you don't want to talk about?"

"Do you think I'm lying?" he asked in a gritty voice. "What do you think—that I whipped some slave and fucked her—and I don't want to tell you about it?"

It took several moments before she answered, "I hope not."

"Jesus!" When he tried to wrench himself away, her grip on his shoulder tightened. Maybe he didn't really want to get away because he flopped back onto the bed. Or maybe he didn't have the strength to escape.

That in itself was terrifying. She'd never seen Cole Marshall like this, and she was realizing how much she'd come to rely on his steady dependability.

"You really don't know?" she murmured, thinking that they were in a very bad situation. In the first place, somebody could be listening to this conversation. Probably they *were* listening. And she'd better keep that in mind.

She thought back over their dialogue. Had they said anything that an ordinary man and woman wouldn't say to each other?

It seemed not. She hoped not.

"But you're still feeling sick?" she murmured.

"It's not so bad now." He swallowed, his hands clenching and unclenching. "The worst part is not knowing how I got this way," he said in a barely audible voice.

She knew what it must have cost him to admit that. Lying down on the bed beside him, she clasped her arm across his chest, holding him tightly.

He kept his eyes closed when he asked, "How long was I gone?"

"Three hours."

"Jesus."

"What's the last thing you remember?"

127

He hesitated, and she wondered if he was dredging up a lie. Yet when he spoke, his answer sounded sincere. "I remember walking down the hall, coming back here. Before that, I remember leaving. In between is a whole lot of unaccounted-for time."

"Where were you going when you left?"

"I was trying to get—" He stopped abruptly and started again, "You know, find out about the ship."

Probably about Karen, but he'd managed not to say it.

"Where did you end up?"

He shook his head. "No idea."

Again, she had the sense that he wasn't being entirely truthful. "You have to try and remember. I mean, what if something happened that . . ."

She let the question trail off. She'd wondered if his experiences had put them in danger, but she certainly couldn't ask that. Instead, she reached down and laid her hand over his. "Maybe I can help you remember."

Cole considered his options. He *could not* tell her about changing to wolf form, killing the guard, getting rid of the body. But could she really help him dredge up the rest of it— the part before?

"How in the hell can you do that?" he demanded in his Cole Mason voice.

"By asking you some questions."

He'd been hoping for some magic bullet. Now he made a snorting sound. "Don't you understand. My memory for those hours is gone. Asking questions won't do any good."

"Maybe it will. Just let me try."

"What are you, a therapist or something?"

"Just someone who cares about you."

He waited several seconds before answering. "Okay."

She got up and dimmed the lights, then came back to the bed, sitting beside him in the semidarkness.

"I'm going to ask you stuff fast. Don't think too hard about it. Don't try to second-guess yourself. Just say the first thing that comes into your mind."

"Where did you get that?"

"From a TV show."

He snorted. Maybe it was really from a police manual.

"I'm going to start. What color was the hallway?"

"The walls are buff."

"What other color do you remember?"

"Green," he said, then stopped short as though the answer had been a revelation.

"What was green?"

"Her dress."

She kept the questions coming fast. "Whose dress?"

"Stella's." He turned to Emma and blinked. "Stella," he said again, remembering. "She was standing in the doorway to the bar. She invited me in. She was being friendly."

"You were talking to her?"

"Yes. About . . ." He stopped and shrugged. "I haven't a clue."

"Was that true, or was he censoring himself?"

"Did you have a drink?"

"I never drink anything stronger than soda water." he snapped, then gasped as another memory flooded in. "The soda water."

"What?"

"I drank it, and it tasted funny." He sat up with a jerk, as another piece of the puzzle slipped into place. "The guy named Ben. He was there."

"In the bar?"

"Not the bar. In a room. Asking me questions."

"What kind of questions?"

"My name. Your name. What I was doing here." He stopped and stared at Emma. "Oh shit. I think the woman put something in the drink to make me tell the truth."

"They drugged you?"

129

Recognizing the import of the question, he felt his heart start to pound.

Emma kept her gaze on him. Punching out the words, she said, "And you obviously did tell the truth. Maybe they do that, you know, at random. Or maybe they went after you because they suspect you of something, but neither one of us had done anything wrong."

"Yeah. Right." After the assertion, he moved his mouth to her ear. "But I put us in danger. Put *you* in danger."

She reversed their positions. "Not your fault. If you'd said something off, we'd already be in custody, don't you think?"

He answered with a grunt. Yeah, that was right, as far as it went. Or maybe the goon squad was waiting to see if he said anything interesting.

Her voice turned hard. Aloud, she said, "I'm going to call up security now and complain about the way they treated you. You're paying through the nose for this vacation. They can't do that to you."

"You think they're going to apologize?" he snapped.

"Maybe."

"Forget it. I need to get some sleep. And you do too."

CHAPTER TWELVE

Alarm shot through Emma as she watched Cole get up and sway like a man who was three sheets to the wind. "What are you doing?"

"Like I said. Getting some sleep," he said in a rough voice. "I believe we have a party tomorrow. It's supposed to be fun, and I'd like to be in shape to enjoy myself."

Enjoy himself. Oh sure she thought as he snatched up pillows and the bedspread. What the heck was he doing?

"Come on," he whispered.

"Where?"

Still not quite steady on his feet, he led her to the side of the room, and threw down the spread. As she helped him smooth it out, she understood his strategy. If someone did come barging in here, they'd go straight for the bed. But nobody would be there.

But then what? Cole was obviously not in shape to fight off Del Conte's security men or anyone else.

As she watched him settle down against the wall, her chest tightened. How bad off was he? And how would he be in the morning? She'd told him that if he'd given anything away in the interrogation, the security men would already be after them. Praying it was true, she got up and walked to the bathroom where she got the knife disguised as a nail file out of her makeup kit.

It was pitifully little protection if the security force attacked, but it was the best she could do. If she could have gotten Cole and herself off the ship right then, she would have done it. But that wasn't an option, not until they'd rescued Karen.

If they could do it.

Hoping they weren't living on borrowed time, she settled down beside Cole.

"Sorry," he murmured.

"Not your fault," she answered, reaching for his hand and linking her fingers with his. She'd been worried sick and angry while he'd been gone. She was still worried about him, and there was nothing she could do.

One of them should stay awake to keep guard. Logically, it should be her, since he obviously needed to rest.

But she was also exhausted. Although she tried to stay awake, she finally dozed off.

Sometime in the small hours of the morning, she woke with a start.

Struggling to get her bearings, she thought that security men had broken into the room. As she prepared to spring up, she realized that Cole was moaning and moving restlessly in his sleep.

"Cole?"

He didn't answer, and she knew he must be dreaming, or reacting to the drugs that the woman had given him. He was saying something she didn't understand. Strange words that made the hair on the back of her neck prickle. Next to her, she felt his body jerk.

"*Taranis, Epona, Cerridwen*," he intoned, then repeated the same phrase and went on to another.

"*Ga. Feart. Cleas. Duais. Aithriocht. Go gcumhdai is dtreorai na deithe thu.*"

The words sounded incredibly ancient. And powerful. How did he know them?

As she listened, they stirred a deep primal fear in the marrow of her bones. They were like nothing she had ever heard—a throwback to a time before written history when the world was a savage place.

A chant or a prayer that might have been passed down through the ages without benefit of written language. They roared through her, almost choking off her breath.

When she put her hand on Cole's shoulder, it didn't feel right. Instead of skin, was she feeling hair? Or fur, or something?

They'd made love. She thought she knew his body, but she didn't remember anything like that.

When his frame jerked as though animated by forces outside his control, fear ripped through her. What in the name of God was going on?

Uncertainty tore at her. She wanted to leap out of bed and turn on the light so she could see him. Maybe she would have done it, if she hadn't been terrified of what she would discover.

Touch was bad enough. Primal instinct made her want to get as far away from him as possible. Instead, she gripped his arm again, shaking him hard.

"Cole?"

He jumped. To her relief, the chant cut off abruptly as he sucked in a breath. But it was clear he was still dreaming. In the darkness, he reared up, coming down on top of her, his hands fastening on her shoulders as though they were antagonists locked in mortal combat.

When he began to shake her hard enough to make her teeth rattle, she choked out, "Cole. It's Emma. Cole. Stop."

It was clear she wasn't getting through. He pinned her to the makeshift bed, his body pressing her down as though his life depended on immobilizing her.

What should she do? Try to fight him off, or go limp?

The first was probably a bad idea—given his superior strength. The latter was terrifying. What was he going to do next?

If she could have clasped him to her and stroked her hands over his back and shoulders as she murmured soothing words, she would have done it. But she couldn't move. Her only option was to keep speaking his name along with her reassurance that everything was all right, as she prayed that she would get through to him before he did her serious damage.

In the darkness, she stared up at him, feeling his breath wheezing in and out. She couldn't see his face, but she knew the moment when he realized who she was.

With a curse, he flopped to his back and lay breathing hard.

"Christ! I was doing it again."

"What?"

"Sorry," he whispered. After a moment, he added, "I must have been having a nightmare. I guess it's the effects of that damn drug."

"It's okay."

"Did I hurt you?"

"No," she lied.

"I think I did. I'm sorry."

"What was the nightmare about?"

He gave a sharp laugh. "About that bastard security guard."

"What guard?"

Again he hesitated as though he was trying to decide what to say. "The one named Ben. He was interrogating me, only this time I got the better of him." He laughed again. "I wish."

She clenched her hand on his arm, as she realized suddenly that someone else might be listening in on the conversation.

In the dark, she pressed her fingers against his lips. With her mouth near his ear, she murmured, "I shouldn't have asked."

He silently nodded.

She clasped his fingers with hers. When she squeezed, he squeezed back. There was so much she wanted to say, but that was impossible here.

Was the danger around them fueling her feelings for him? Probably, but she knew it was more than that.

She ached to ask what she meant to him. In the darkness, she could only hang on to his hand.

Ben poured himself a cup of coffee from the dispenser at the side of the operations room, then played the recording again. Every time he heard Cole Mason chant, it raised goose bumps on his arms. It was weird. And rendered with an unnerving sincerity.

"What is it?" Greg asked. Since Mason had escaped, he'd been listening in on the bedroom where the guy and his honey were holed up. He'd heard the conversation, called the security chief in, and played the recording again.

Ben gestured toward a computer screen. "I've looked up the words. I think they're ancient Celtic."

"What do they mean?"

"I think he's asking the gods for powers."

Greg snorted. "You're kidding, right?"

Ben shrugged. "That's the best I can come up with."

"A lot of good the ancient gods are going to do him here."

They played the recording again.

"Could it be some kind of code?" Greg asked.

"I guess it could be," Ben acknowledged. "But he seemed to be dreaming when he said it. At least that's what he told Emma."

"If he was telling the truth." Greg sighed. "He said he was interested in ancient Greece and Rome,"

"And Druids."

"What if he belongs to some ancient cult?"

Ben shrugged again. "I guess that's possible."

"If it's not a code, what other explanation is there for that freaky chant.?"

"I don't know."

"You think we should wake up the boss?"

"You want to wake him up for *that*?"

Greg thought about it. "I guess not."

"We'll keep an eye on them at the ceremony."

"If he's in shape to get there."

"I'll bet you he does. He's tough. Even drugged, he packed a wallop."

Greg nodded. "Yeah, he struck me as a macho guy who wouldn't want anyone to know he was hurting, but you never know how a person will react to drugs."

Cole woke. Lying very still, he catalogued his faculties. And his memories.

Last night Emma, bless her, had done something that he'd thought was impossible. With her questions, she'd brought back the memories of the interrogation session. At least he knew what had happened during those missing hours. Or the parts where he hadn't been passed out.

If he wasn't fooling himself—and her—he hadn't given the mission away, although he couldn't be absolutely sure. Which was making his pulse pound. He still half expected armed men to come charging through the door.

He turned his head and saw that Emma was also awake, and looking at him in the dim light filtering in around the shades.

"How do you feel?" she asked, reaching up to lay her hand against his cheek. He turned his head and kissed her palm.

"Almost human." It was a joke that she couldn't get. Not yet. He could give that answer every morning of his life.

She moved closer, and he wrapped his arm around her shoulder, drawing her close, wanting her and at the same time knowing that they couldn't get very deep into anything personal now.

When she slid her lips along his cheek, he fought the urge to turn his head again.

Maybe she was reading his thoughts when she murmured, "I know we can't make love, but could you just hold me."

He drew her in closer, closing his eyes, wishing they were somewhere else. Wishing he could tell her all the things that he was hiding.

As they lay together, he felt arousal wrapping them together. When he thought it would overwhelm him, he eased away, regret in his eyes.

"I know," she murmured.

Gingerly he sat up and was pleased to find that the room wasn't spinning around him.

When he saw that Emma was watching him carefully, he said, "We've got a party this morning. Another special treat from our host," he added, trying not to sound too sarcastic.

"Maybe we should skip it," she answered.

The suggestion was tempting. He wanted to get Karen off the boat before it was too late. But that wasn't going to be so easy. Suppose he skipped the party. Then what? His mishap with Stella and Big Ben had put him on the *Windward* radar screen. He wasn't going to feel like he could sneeze without the security force knowing about it.

And speaking of security, by now they must know the guy he'd killed was missing. The best case scenario was that they thought he'd joined the rebels or whoever they were. Or maybe he'd gotten off the ship.

Yeah, off the ship. Floating in the ocean.

"We're paying good money for this vacation, and I want to enjoy it," he said punching out the words. Maybe Karen would be at the party. Maybe that was the special attraction, and Del Conte wanted to test his reaction. At least he could hope she'd be there. And then what?

Emma answered his spoken comment with a tight nod, then said brightly, "While you were gone, I was looking at some of the information about the ship. There's a deluxe breakfast buffet on Deck Three. Everything from bacon and eggs to Belgian waffles."

"Yum. As good a place as any to eat before the party."

At considerable risk to himself, a man slipped into a storage room in the maintenance area of the ship. He had urgent business with one of the women who also worked on the *Windward*.

They had met in person only a few times, but this was an emergency situation.

Because the luxury liner was an environment full of cameras and listening devices, they had to be extremely careful. But they'd both been on the ship long enough to know how to avoid the worst pitfalls. They hoped.

This morning he was dressed in the gray overalls worn by the crew members who kept the ship running smoothly. He'd left his quarters carrying small canvas bags with the overalls and had found a spot outside of camera range to pull on the disguise over his clothing. And he'd made sure that the monitoring system in the seldom used storage room had been disabled long ago.

The meeting had been arranged through a dead drop on Deck Five where a section of paneling in a hallway had been loosened enough to hold a thin slip of paper. With a cryptic message that wouldn't get anyone tortured or killed if it was discovered.

The man had left a request to the woman, asking for the meeting. He couldn't be absolutely sure she'd picked up the note. But he was hoping for the best.

He arrived first, his nerves jumping as he waited in the darkened room for the other party to show up. She might or might not make the meeting, depending on her duties and how comfortable she felt slipping away.

That was the worst part about this damn environment. People were always watching you, even people you thought were your friends. They might be spies. Or they might be out to curry favor with Del Conte by reporting suspicious behavior.

The man and the woman were not exactly allies, but they had found it useful to communicate on matters of mutual interest. Perhaps that was becoming too dangerous in the current environment.

There were too many unknowns now, including the wild card that had introduced itself recently.

He stood in the dark, ordering himself not to pace back and forth while the minutes ticked by. He couldn't stay here all day. He had to report to duty.

He was about to leave when she finally slipped into the room, emitting a thin shaft of light from the corridor before closing the door behind her.

"What the hell is going on?" he asked. "Don't you know that the stunts your group is pulling could get us all killed?"

"I'm sorry. The frustration level is so high . . ." Her voice trailed off.

He wished he could see her face, but it was safer to remain in the dark. "Did your group kill a security guard last night?"

"What?"

"Tom Dalhasi."

"He was a sick bastard, but we didn't go after him. What happened?"

"I don't know. I found out a while ago that he's missing." The conspirator dragged in a breath and let it out. "You know I'm as committed to stopping Del Conte as you are. But creating chaos among the guests isn't the way."

139

In the darkness, she stepped toward him and put a hand on his arm. "I'll convey that message."

"You've lost control of the group. Maybe one of them offed Dalhasi as a solo project."

"It's possible."

He waited a beat before saying. "There may be someone on the ship that can help us."

"Who?"

"I think you've got a pretty good idea."

"Yes," she murmured. "Maybe they did Dalhasi."

"That's possible. Meanwhile, try to talk some sense into your people."

"If I can."

"Tell the hotheads they'll get us all killed."

"Not you."

"You can never be sure."

"Unfortunately. I'd better go, before I'm missed. I have an assignment in a little while."

She left first. He gave her a ten-minute head start, then exited the room and returned to his duties, wondering if she was lying about Dalhasi.

While he showered and shaved, Cole kept evaluating his options—and his condition. He still didn't know how the hell he and Emma were going to complete the assignment. They didn't even know if Karen was still in the Tropical Lounge. If Del Conte was worried about a rebellion on the ship, maybe he'd moved her to a more secure location.

He sighed. Nobody had understood how impossible this situation was when Frank Decorah had sent them here. They would have had a better chance with a surprise attack by a raiding party. If they'd known where to find Karen. Now Cole was thinking they'd be lucky to get out alive—let alone with Karen Hopewell.

Unable to come up with firm plans, he switched to evaluating his condition. It felt like he was operating at about eighty percent of normal capacity. Not great, but it would have to do. And they would have to find Karen. Before it was too late.

Wondering about the party attire, he dressed in jeans and a knit shirt. Before they left the room, he gave Emma a confident smile. She smiled back, but he knew that they were both prepared for trouble as he opened the door.

He counted it a good sign when no one was waiting in the hall with machine guns pointed in their direction.

There were a couple of dozen guests in the elegantly furnished room where breakfast was laid out on long tables spread with crisp white cloths. A few single men were scattered around the room, but most were at tables for two. Nobody was striking up conversations with the other guests. Or making eye contact with anyone besides their breakfast companion, if they had one. If he had to evaluate the mood of the room, he'd call it subdued. Not like a bunch of people anticipating a good time.

Maybe the gunshots and the attacks were getting to the guests. What if some of them wanted to go home? Would Del Conte let them, or would he insist that they stay—and pay—for the days they'd booked?

He and Emma found a table near the window where they could look out at the ocean.

"What a beautiful view," she chirped as she spread peach jam and cream cheese on a toasted bagel."

"Stunning," he agreed, then took a bite of the rare steak he'd served himself.

But it was hard to sit there and choke down food. Cole kept his eye out for anyone paying particular attention to him and Emma, but as far as he could tell, no one was going to arrest him while he ate. He'd filled his plate not because he was hungry but because he figured he needed the fuel.

When they were almost finished eating, two of the cast members came up to their table. They were dressed in uniforms, the guy like an English butler in a dark suit, crisp white shirt and vest. The woman was outfitted like a French maid with a short black dress, white apron and black fishnet stockings.

"Cole Mason and Emma Ray?" the butler asked. He looked to be in his thirties, with bleached blond hair.

He and Emma both tensed, although they were both trying to look casual.

"Yes," he answered.

"It's our pleasure to get you ready for the party."

The woman stepped forward and held out her hand to Emma. "I'm Francine. I'll take care of you."

The butler walked to Cole. "I am Sidney. Let me show you to your dressing room suite."

"We're separating?" Emma asked in a voice she couldn't quite hold steady.

"To the men's and women's dressing areas. You'll meet again at the party," Sidney said.

"Okay," Cole answered, allowing the butler to lead him through the door. He wanted to look back at Emma, but he kept his gaze straight ahead.

This could be some kind of trick. A ploy to get him away from the other guests before they grabbed him.

Maybe, but in the Tropical Lounge the security staff hadn't been shy about grabbing anyone.

CHAPTER THIRTEEN

With a sick feeling in the pit of her stomach, Emma followed Francine down a long hallway.

After last night, she hated being separated from Cole. What if they were going to interrogate him the way they had last night? And this dressing room thing was just a way to get him off alone? Or maybe it was her they wanted to interrogate?

That fear wasn't the only thing making her stomach churn. She'd seen Karen in that cell. Seen her see-through outfit and the terror on the girl's face. But at least she'd looked unharmed. No bruises or obvious signs of ill treatment.

Francine stopped at an elevator and pressed the button.

"Have you been to these parties?" Emma asked.

"Yes."

"Did you have a good time?"

The woman hesitated, looking uneasy. "The guests have a good time."

"It's no fun for you?"

"The fun is for the guests. The staff does their job."

Emma waited a moment before taking a chance on saying, "I saw a woman in a cage. Is she a guest? Or does she work here?"

"I didn't see her," Francine snapped. "Please, stop asking so many questions." She lowered her voice. "Are you trying to get me in trouble."

"No," Emma answered, pretty sure she wasn't going to get any useful information and sorry if she really had made trouble for the woman.

The elevator took them to Deck Two where they followed another corridor to what could have been the fitting room in an upscale department store.

Francine gestured toward one of the cubicles. "Go in and take off all your clothes."

"Everything?"

"Yes, the costuming for the party is authentic. No modern underwear.

Emma nodded tightly. Inside the dressing room, she pulled off her sundress and hung it on a hanger. She had on no bra. After a moment's hesitation, she took off her sandals, then pulled down her panties and stepped out of them.

Francine knocked on the door, then entered, holding a box full of clothing and taking an appraising look at Emma's body.

"You have a good figure."

"Thank you," she answered, resisting the desire to fold her arms across her breasts.

"And it looks like you keep yourself in shape."

"Yes. I jog. And rock climb."

"Don't neglect the weight machines. We have an excellent gym and trainers on the ship."

"Okay."

Francine handed her a garment. "It's a tunic. It buttons up the front. And there's a skirt."

Emma slipped the tunic on, then the skirt, noting that the lower garment barely covered her naked ass. The neckline dipped low in front, skimming the tops of her breasts. Turquoise dyed feather epaulets decorated each shoulder. As she fastened the row of buttons down the front, she said, "The Maya wore these?"

"I wouldn't know. I only get the costumes requested."

"Right."

The footwear was soft leather boots with rows of ruffles around the ankles.

Finally, Francine helped her attach a decorative headdress.

"You look lovely," the woman approved.

Emma studied herself in the full-length mirror. "I feel like I'm going to a costume party."

"You are. You'll fit right in."

"What do they do there?"

"It depends?"

"An orgy," she asked, her chest tightening as she wondered how she'd get through something like that.

"Probably not."

At least that was something.

They exited the dressing room into another hallway. "It's two doors down on the right. Have a wonderful time."

"Thanks." With her heart in her throat, Emma walked toward the doorway. Beyond she could hear soft drumming and flute music, also people laughing and talking.

She pushed the door open and stepped into another world.

The room was large. The tropical greenery on two sides was similar to where they'd been earlier. But there the resemblance ended.

Blue light obscured the ceiling and gave the room an eerie cast. High walls of what looked like rough-cut stone enclosed the space. At the far end was a pyramid with primitive drawings carved into the stone.

The place had a strange, ancient quality, making her feel like she'd journeyed back in time. And the air was thick with the scent of incense or perhaps something stronger. Which wouldn't be out of keeping with Mayan rituals she remembered from some of her reading in college.

About fifteen men and women were scattered around the area, all dressed in outfits similar to her own. Only the men had one-piece tunics, and the women had a top and skirt. Some men and women seemed to be couples. Others were alone and scanning the crowd.

"Welcome," a man dressed like an ancient warrior and holding a spear intoned. "The ceremony will begin shortly." He wore a bird-like mask, and his outfit was a bit more elaborate than the others, with a gold necklace and a jeweled belt.

She took a step forward, looking around anxiously for Cole but didn't spot him. The atmosphere in the room made her nerves jangle. She sensed arousal. Anticipation. Excitement.

Oh Lord, suppose she and Cole were really separated for the day? Had he been sent to some other party by mistake—or on purpose. Or did his absence signify something worse?

She wanted to exit the room, but that wasn't an option.

While she was debating what to do, a waiter, also in Mayan dress came around with a tray of ceramic cups.

To give herself something to do, she took one and murmured a thanks. One sip told her she wouldn't be drinking much. It was potent, perhaps a rum punch that was mostly liquor. Or did it have something else in it—like what they'd given to Cole last night? She shuddered, hoping that wasn't going to happen to her.

An uncomfortable feeling made her glance up to find a man eyeing her, his gaze lingering on her breasts and her hips before gliding upward to her face. He was tall, over six feet, and looked to be in his early fifties, with salt and pepper hair cut short. Smiling, he came toward her.

"Hello. I'm Dane."

"Emma," she answered.

"Your first time here?"

She moistened her lips before answering and knew he followed the movement of her tongue. "Yes."

When he stepped closer, she took a small step back.

"Are you alone?"

She looked around. "My boyfriend is supposed to be here."

"Maybe he changed his mind."

"He wouldn't do that," she answered, praying she'd see him soon.

The drumming and flute music swirled around her. The man stepped closer, putting a hand on her arm, stroking.

"I'm spoken for," she said.

"We'll see."

She could coldcock him, but then she would be stepping completely out of character.

"That tunic looks wonderful on you," he said, reaching out to stroke a hand against her breast.

She caught her breath, trying to back away and found that he was crowding her into a corner.

"Don't."

"You'll find me a very good lover. If you accept my discipline."

She tensed, caught between her need to escape and her need to maintain her cover. What if Del Conte was watching to see what she'd do?

She was saved from making a decision when a harsh voice said, "Sorry I'm late, sweetie,"

Relief washed over Emma. It was Cole.

"It's all right. I just got here," she said, knowing that if she told him what had happened, this guy was dog meat.

Dane must have come to a similar conclusion because he moved quickly away.

"What took you so long?" she asked, struggling to hold her voice steady.

"The first set of clothing Sidney brought me was too tight."

147

She nodded, wondering if that had been on purpose so she'd have to start out here alone.

"Then when I didn't see you, I went looking and found that guy had pushed you into a corner."

"Yes."

The drums and flutes suddenly stopped, and the whole room went silent.

Everybody was turning expectantly toward Emma's right, and she looked to see two men dressed in feathered, flowing robes and huge headdresses step into the room. Between them was a slender blond young woman, her face a mixture of panic and excitement.

She was dressed in a white gown, a bit like one of those hotel bathrobes only much thinner so that her naked body showed through the fabric.

The priests led her across the room, through the crowd toward a narrow stone table Emma hadn't seen earlier.

Everybody followed, making a circle around the table. Emma and Cole hung a little back. Whatever was going to happen, she didn't want to see much of it.

"We are here to worship the ancient gods in the ways that have been handed down through the ages."

"Yes," the crowd answered.

"And one among us with grace and strength will be our offering."

The priest looked at the woman. "We thank you for surrendering to the ancient gods. Do you give yourself freely?"

"Yes," she murmured.

One of the priests handed her a cup, and she drank from it, grimacing a little before handing it back.

"We will begin. Take off your gown," he said.

Her hands weren't quite steady as she fumbled with the belt at her waist, untying it, then pulling the gown open and shrugging it off her shoulders so that it pooled around her ankles. She had narrow hips and big breasts, and her pubic hair had been shaved.

As she stood naked for a moment before the assembled men and women, a buzz of anticipation rose around the room.

"Climb onto the table and submit."

She mounted a short set of steps to the horizontal surface and lay down with her arms at her sides. One of the priests pulled her hands above her head and fastened them to a metal ring. Her hips were near the end of the table, and the other priest spread her legs so that they were hanging over the sides, where small platforms supported her feet. When she was secured to the table, one of the priests stepped back, and the other began to murmur low, sensual words in a foreign language as he started to stroke her with a wand made of long feathers. He stroked her arms, her ribs, the sides of her breasts, and she stirred on the table, obviously aroused by the feathery touch.

He slid the feathers along the insides of her thighs, then came back to her breasts, drawing wide then increasingly narrow circles around her nipples, until the feathers were rubbing against the raised crests. Emma could hear her harsh breathing.

From the side of the table he picked up two metal clips, opening and closing them, clacking them together.

Then he took one of her nipples between his fingers, pulling and tugging on it before opening the metal and clipping it onto her breast, behind the nipple so that it stood up higher.

Lord, didn't that hurt? Or was she accustomed to this kind of treatment?

She cried out as he played with the crest of the nipple before repeating the procedure with her other breast.

Both nipples stood up now, held by the clips, The first priest stepped back and the other moved to the end of the table, dipping his fingers in scented oil before playing with her genitals, pulling on her labia, making brief passes at her clit, thrusting one finger inside her and stroking slowly in and out of her vagina, making the woman on the table writhe.

Emma was horrified at the scene, yet she couldn't stop herself from reacting. Watching the priests turn this woman on was turning her on, too.

The woman raised and lowered her hips in a frantic motion.

"Do you need sexual satisfaction?" the priest asked.

"Yes," she gasped.

"It's much too soon. Your satisfaction will be your offering to the gods. But you must be worthy to give it." His partner played with her nipples again, brushing over the stiffened tips above the clips.

"Please," she gasped. When she tried to rock her hips, he placed a hand on her thigh, holding her still as he played with the entrance to her vagina, circling his finger just inside the rim.

She moaned.

He picked up a curved ivory-colored rod from the side of the table, oiled it and held it up for the crowd to see. Turning back to the woman, he slipped it into her anus, stroking in and out.

"Jesus," Cole swore.

He put his hand on Emma's arm, pulling her away from the scene, leading her toward one of the stone walls.

She hadn't noticed that there were wooden plank doors in the wall, but he opened one, leading her into a small bedroom.

He slammed the door behind them and gathered her into his arms, lowering his mouth to hers for a savage kiss.

After the tension of the night before, it was a release of all the emotions they'd been holding in check.

She clung to him, giving and taking.

Kissing wasn't enough. She was ravenous for more. When one of his hands slid down to her hips, pulling her lower body against his enormous erection, she moved against him, frustrated that he was hitting her middle and not where she needed him.

With undisguised greed, he slipped his other hand between them and cupped one breast, taking the weight of it in his palm, and she knew she had been wanting him to touch her like that since the last time they'd made love.

As he stroked his thumb over the hardened tip, she heard herself make a low, pleading sound. When he tugged at her tunic, she helped him get it over her head. He tossed it away, then lowered his head, circling her nipple with his tongue before sucking it into his mouth and pulling on her strongly.

The sensations made her drunk with need. And she tried to tell him by arching into the caress.

His kiss turned frantic as his hands moved over her body, pulling off her short shirt, stroking her hips, her arms, and back to her breasts.

Her hands were no less frantic as they worked at his tunic, dispatching it as he had dispatched hers until he was naked in her arms.

The feel of his skin against hers drove her almost to madness.

His hands slid down her back, over the curve of her bottom, pulling her against himself.

Reaching up, she pulled his head down to hers, kissing him with a passion born of need—and fear for the future. They were in a horrible place where anything could happen. They had an assignment to complete. And for a moment their mission intruded.

"We have work to do."

"We can't do it now."

When he lifted her in his arms and carried her to the bed, she wondered if he was afraid that she'd try to break away from him.

Never!

He laid her down gently, then came down on top of her, panting as he trailed kisses down her throat, then her collarbones, working his way to her breasts, turning his head one way and then the other, kissing and licking at her, driving her wild with need.

His hand slid down her body, then into the triangle of blond hair at the top of her legs before reaching lower to glide into her sex. She was swollen and slick for him, and he murmured his appreciation as he stroked her from vagina to clit and back again.

"Please. I want you inside me."

"My finger?"

"Are you teasing me—the way the priests were teasing that woman?"

"Did that turn you on. Watching her?"

"You know it did. And you know it's more than that. It's us. Together."

He moved over her, angling his body so that his penis slid against her wet heat.

Unable to wait, she took his firm, full cock in her hand and guided him to her vagina.

And then, finally, finally, he was inside her, filling her.

She kept her hands on his back as he bent to kiss her, then began to move his hips, drawing almost all the way out of her, before gliding back in, the measured rhythm teasing and inciting her.

"Please . . ." she moaned, like the woman on the table, her hips raising and lowering, begging him to speed up his strokes.

As the pace became frantic, she climbed toward the top of a high mountain, where the thin air made her head spin. And as she toppled over the edge, she felt him follow her into space.

He clasped her to him, calling out her name as his body jerked with his climax.

He lay on top of her, breathing hard, then shifted to his side, taking her with him, clasping her sweat-slick body.

She belonged to him in ways she had never imagined. Maybe she had belonged to him since the day they'd met. And he belonged to her.

"We have to talk," he said in a voice that sent a shiver down her spine.

"About us?"

"Yeah. I have to tell you things about me."

"Something I'm not going to like?"

"I wish I knew."

At that moment, the door burst open and armed men spilled into the room.

Emma cried out.

CHAPTER FOURTEEN

Emma cried out.

Cole leaped off the bed, putting himself between the men and Emma, but he knew that if he attacked, they'd kill him, and do God knew what to her.

"Don't move, or you're dead." It was the guy named Greg who had served them drinks on the hovercraft. He looked a lot less friendly now.

"Hands behind your backs."

"Let her put some clothes on," Cole growled, keeping his voice steady when he wanted to scream in rage. How dare these bastards burst into a private bedroom.

But he knew they wouldn't have done it unless they'd found out something about him and Emma. Had he said something last night, and they'd been waiting to pounce.? Or was there some other source of information? The question was, how much did they know?

He saw the men ogling Emma's naked body as she cringed away and tried to cover herself. Their smirking faces made him want to crash their heads together, but somehow he kept from going berserk.

After an eternity of silence, Greg picked the tunic up off the floor and threw it at Emma. She snatched it up and pulled it over her head. It covered her from shoulders to just under her breasts, leaving most of her exposed. She was less than half dressed, and that looked like that was all she was going to get.

"Hands behind your back," Greg said again.

Still buck naked, Cole complied, and the security man clamped metal cuffs around his wrists.

Another man did the same for Emma. Her eyes met Cole's, and he saw the panic that she was struggling to hold down.

He wanted to say something reassuring, but it would only be a lie. They were in bad trouble.

"We are going through the party room to the exit. Walk straight ahead. Keep your eyes down. Don't try anything funny."

They exited the bedroom to find everyone craning their necks to get a look at them. Cole was still naked, and he knew that was an intimidation tactic. On the other hand, it probably wasn't all that unusual on this damn ship.

The security men had told them to look down, but Cole kept his head up, his gaze raking the crowd as the armed men marched them through the fantasy setting and out the door.

They formed a parade down the hallway with a guard in front, Emma next, then Cole and two more security men.

He kept trying to figure out how to get away, but he couldn't think of anything that wouldn't get them shot. Or worse.

They all took the elevator to Deck Five and then to Del Conte's office.

The *Windward*'s master was sitting behind his desk his face impassive. But Cole saw emotions churning below the surface of his calm. Although he looked the captives up and down appraisingly, Cole refused to be intimidated.

"What's this about?" he demanded.

"Your background doesn't check out."

"I don't believe that."

Ignoring the protest, Del Conte continued, "Why are you really here?"

"To have a good time."

"What's your real name?"

"Cole Mason."

"I don't think so."

Cole wanted to ask if he'd given Big Ben the wrong answers, but then he'd be admitting that there *were* wrong ones.

Del Conte kept his gaze steady. "Did you kill one of my security officers, a man named Tom Dalhasi."

Emma sucked in a sharp breath, her gaze going to Cole.

He kept his voice even. "No."

"He went missing last night. There's a bloodstain on the carpet in one of the staterooms."

Remembering the injured woman from last night, Cole snapped, "Maybe one of your guests got too rough with a slave."

Del Conte glared at him. "Don't be ridiculous."

No point in challenging him on that. "You have any evidence linking me to him?"

"A man in a security officer's uniform dumped a heavy bundle off the side of the ship around 3:00 a.m."

Cole shook his head. "I don't know anything about it." He looked at Emma. "I was with you then, wasn't I?"

"Yes," she managed to say.

"You got back at three twenty," Del Conte said.

Emma was watching the exchange wide-eyed. Obviously she was thinking about last night, reevaluating what he'd said about the missing hours.

Del Conte kept his voice even. "I believe you'll tell me what I want to know."

"I have told you!" Cole spat out as he glared at the man.

The master of the *Windward* leaned back comfortably in his expensive desk chair. "You'd rather watch me torture Ms.

Ray? I can tie her to that stone table in the party room and do some things that she's not going to like."

Cole's guts twisted. He'd talk to save Emma. The problem was, he was pretty sure that talking wasn't going to buy them much. Once Del Conte found out why they were here, they'd both end up buried at sea like Tom Dalhasi.

Del Conte looked at Emma. "Did you go to the Carlton Academy in Baltimore?"

She stared at him. "No."

"Where did you go to school?"

After a slight hesitation, she answered, "Woodrow Wilson High School."

"We can check on that. I'll give you some time to think about it," he said. "A half hour." He turned to Greg. "Lock them in the brig."

The guards marched them out of the office and down the hall again, into an anteroom with a desk, several chairs, a row of lockers, and a computer system with a bank of monitors showing various views of the ship. Also a gun rack with Uzis along the wall. Well, maybe things were looking up.

There were doors along a hallway, and Greg shoved him through one into a metal room about ten by twelve. Emma landed on top of him before the door slammed closed behind them.

He took a moment to catch his breath and assess their surroundings before scooting around so that Emma was leaning against him.

"I'm so sorry," he whispered.

"Did you kill that guy?"

"If I had, I wouldn't tell you about it now."

She looked around the room. "Yeah. They're probably hoping we'll say something incriminating in here. She forced a laugh. "Like where I went to school; can you believe he asked about that?"

He leaned over to press his cheek to hers and spoke in a barely audible voice. "He must have some idea about your background."

"How?"

"No idea. But we'll get out of this."

"How?"

An plan was forming in his mind. A desperate idea he wouldn't consider under any other circumstances.

"Emma, look at me." He ached to take her in his arms, but his hands were secured behind his back. Pulling away, he saw tears glistening in her eyes.

There was something he had to tell her. Something important.

"I love you. I couldn't admit that—even to myself. Maybe I was trying to run away from it last night, but I've known it was true since we first made love."

"Oh Cole. I knew it too. I love you. So much."

He swallowed hard. "No way am I going to let them torture you."

"I don't think you can stop them."

Ignoring the comment he continued, "There's something you need to know."

"What?"

He looked up again, scanning the room and shook his head. "You're going to have to trust me."

"I do."

"You may not. In a while. But . . ." He moved so that his mouth was against her ear. "There's only one way we're going to get out of here."

"Okay," she mouthed.

He closed his eyes for a moment, thinking that this all depended on split-second timing. Otherwise, he was going to dislocate his shoulders.

He wished he could turn off the lights. He wished they'd put him in a separate cell so she wouldn't see him transform for the first time like this. But he had to work with what he had.

He spoke in a low voice, trying to warn her without giving anything away to the men who were listening. "Remember outside the Temptation Club, we split up. And you saw a dog mauling the guy who came after us?"

"Yes."

"Did you think it might be a wolf?"

"I . . . yes."

He gave a sharp laugh. "And then last night when I was chanting in my sleep. Those are clues."

"To what?"

"Clues you're going to need in a few minutes."

She stared at him, and he knew she was wondering if he had come unhinged. Maybe from his ordeal the night before.

"Cole?"

"It's going to work out okay," he said, hoping he wasn't lying through his pointed teeth.

When she started to speak again, he shook his head. "Time's almost up. I have to listen for them coming back."

She nodded.

He gave her a fierce look. "You'd better get up and stand against the wall. As far as you can get from me."

When she didn't move, he prodded. "Go."

Awkwardly, she pushed herself up and moved against the wall, staring at him.

His stomach clenched. He was planning to terrify the men who came to get them. And it wouldn't be much better for Emma. For all she knew, he might be planning to eat her alive.

But he couldn't worry about such details now. Straining his ears, he listened. At first, there was nothing to hear besides the sound of his own harsh breathing—and hers. And he wondered if Del Conte had been lying about his intentions. Finally Cole detected footsteps coming back. Two pairs. Good. He could take care of two men.

"They're coming. Get ready."

"For what?"

"To stay out of the way."

In a low voice he began to chant the ancient words that had transformed the men of his family back into the mists of time.

"*Taranis, Epona, Cerridwen,*" he intoned, then repeated the same phrase and went on to another.

"*Ga. Feart. Cleas. Duais. Aithriocht. Go gcumhdai is dtreorai na deithe thu.*"

Those were the words she'd heard him speak last night.

"Cole?" across the room, Emma's voice was high and strained.

His only option was to ignore her and keep chanting. If he didn't do this right, both of them would be in worse shape than they were now.

He focused on the chant and the change that it brought to his body.

The first few times he'd done it as a teenager had been a nightmare of torture and terror. But once he'd understood what to expect, he'd learned to ride above the physical sensations of bones crunching, muscles jerking, cells transforming from one shape to another.

Thick gray hair formed along his flanks, covering his body in a silver-tipped pelt. The color—the very structure—of his eyes changed as he waited for the exact right moment and pulled his paws from the cuffs that held them, freeing himself.

With a growl of satisfaction, he dropped to all fours. No longer a man but an animal far more suited to the forest than this cell.

He heard Emma scream. He heard the door open, and he leaped at the men who were expecting a couple of naked, cringing captives.

Surprise was on his side. Within seconds, he ripped out the throat of the first guard, then took down the next one, tearing off his gun hand. As blood spurted, he said the chant in his head, changing back to his human form.

He had been a wolf for less than a minute, and changing back so quickly made his head spin and his stomach heave. Unlike last night, he kept from throwing up.

Naked, blood dripping from his mouth, he looked back at Emma who stared at him in shock and disbelief.

"I couldn't tell you," he gasped out. "Not here. It had to be a surprise—for them."

Fumbling in the guard's pocket, he pulled out the key and held it up.

"I've got to get the cuffs off you." He hurried toward her, watching her try to back away along the wall.

"Cole?"

"Yeah," he answered. "Cole Marshall. The same guy who made love to you. The guy who loves you. Only with a few extra attributes that I don't talk about so much."

She only stared at him.

"We have to get out of here. Before we're back up shit creek in a wire canoe. Turn around."

She turned, and he unlocked the cuffs, feeling her flinch.

"What are you?" she asked in a quavering voice.

He wanted to take her in his arms and hold her, stroke her, kiss her. He wanted to explain everything to her and hope to hell she didn't walk away, but there was no time for anything personal now. "Your mate."

"What?"

"We can't talk about it now!"

"We have to."

"If we get out of here alive."

In his plush office, Bruno Del Conte stared at the blank bank of monitors. There had been a flicker of *something*. Then the screen had gone to black.

"What the fuck happened?" he asked as his security chief, Ben Walker, charged into the room.

"The whole system is down."

"I repeat. What the fuck happened?"

"We don't know."

"You have someone working on it?"

"Yes." Ben cleared his throat. "Something happened in the brig, just before the failure."

"What?"

"The picture was out of focus."

Del Conte picked up the phone on his desk and punched in a code.

"The men I sent down there aren't answering. Take a squad to the brig with you. I want Morgan and Ray secured." He thought of other problems. "And make sure all the guests are in their cabins. Tell them . . ." He stopped, wondering what the hell he was going to say.

"The P.A. system isn't working, either."

"Then use your men to inform everyone. Tell them there's an emergency, and we want to make sure nobody gets hurt. But make Morgan and Ray a priority."

"Do you want them alive?"

"I wanted to question them, but at this point, I don't give a shit what happens to them."

"We have to get out of the brig before Del Conte captures us again. More men are probably on the way down here now," Cole bit out.

As he spoke, he charged into the anteroom and pulled an Uzi off the wall. After checking the clip, he raked bullets across the computer control panel, the smell of burning electrical wiring mixing with the smell of the powder.

"Hopefully, that will knock out the monitors on the ship," he called over his shoulder, then began opening lockers. In the second one he found a guard's uniform. The pants fit him reasonably well, and he pulled them on.

When he turned, Emma had taken an Uzi off the rack.

Her face was grim as she bit out, "Just before they captured us, you said we had to talk. Was that wolf stuff what you had in mind?"

"Yeah."

"You could have told me *before* you slept with me."

"Oh sure."

He wanted to make her remember what they meant to each other. But there was no time for a personal discussion. Instead, he kept opening doors. The third locker over had another uniform. "Want some pants?" he asked.

"Yes." She put down the gun long enough to pull on the trousers and roll up the cuffs.

When he heard running feet in the hall, he moved to the side of the door. As a guard rushed in, he bashed the guy over the head with the Uzi.

"Do we have a plan?" Emma asked.

"Get to our main mission," he said, hoping that Del Conte didn't have a clue what that was. They'd invaded his ship, but for all he knew, they could be federal agents trying to stop the slave traffic on the *Windward*.

He stepped to the door and opened it. The corridor was clear.

"Come on."

They'd gotten only about fifty feet from the brig when he heard men running.

He swore under his breath and started opening doors along the corridor. Most were locked, but one was open, and he was about to press Emma inside when four men came around the corner. The one in back was Ben Walker, the security chief.

The men in front of him raised their guns.

Before any of them got off a shot, Walker began to fire, cutting them down from behind in a move that had Cole's jaw gaping open.

As the men fell, Walker dropped his gun and raised his hands. "Don't shoot. I'm on your side."

"What the hell?"

"Long story. Do you remember the interrogation last night?"

"Yes."

"I thought so—from the questions Emma asked you."

Cole's voice turned hard. "You were listening."

"We don't have much time. When I hit you last night, it was to wake you up."

Cole thought about that. "Yeah. It seemed like the wrong move."

"I take it you want to get out of here."

"Why are you helping us?" he asked.

"My sister disappeared into this hellhole. I came here to get her back and found out she was dead."

"And now you're security chief."

"I got here by applying for the job. I had the qualifications."

Cole started to ask another question, but Walker shook his head.

"Later. Right now, we've got to get off the ship."

"Not without Karen Hopewell, the girl in the cage in the Tropical Lounge."

"The rich kid whose father has a beef with Del Conte?"

"Yes."

"Getting to her complicates things."

"We're here to rescue her from this hellhole, as you put it. And we're not leaving without her," Emma said.

"Okay. It's your funeral." He gave Cole a speculative look. "Are you going to tell me what I saw in the brig?"

"Maybe later."

"Did I see . . . a wolf?"

Cole didn't bother denying it.

"I made sure it didn't show up on the evening news."

"Appreciate that," Cole acknowledged.

"And the bloodstain in the cabin? That was your work, too."

"Uh huh."

They were already on their way, bypassing the elevator and heading for the stairs. When they reached Deck Five, Walker motioned them back.

"Give me your weapons."

"Like hell," Cole answered.

"Think about it. If I look like I've captured you, nobody's going to know the difference, until it's too late."

Cole looked at Emma, and she nodded. Again, he didn't like it, but he couldn't see a better alternative.

Walker slung the other two weapons over his shoulder and the three of them stepped out of the stairway, then hurried toward the Tropical Lounge.

The place had been full of men and women having a good time. Now it was deserted.

Completely.

The cage was empty.

CHAPTER FIFTEEN

"Christ. Now what?" Cole turned to Walker

"I assume she's in a more secure location."

"You know where?"

"I hope so."

He was leading them around the cage and toward another exit when the door they'd come through burst open and more armed men charged in.

Cole acted instinctively, stepping in front of Emma, grabbing one of the Uzis from Walker's shoulder and starting to fire.

Two of the men went down. A third took cover behind the bar.

Emma pushed forward, grabbed the other weapon and dodged back behind a large planter.

Walker and Cole joined her.

When Cole heard the man behind the bar using a walkie-talkie to call for backup, he swore.

"How long will it take reinforcements to get here?" he asked the security chief.

"A few minutes. Depending on where they're located—and how busy they are. I took down the PA system, too. Which means some of them are busy getting the guests back to their rooms. And the rebels may be taking advantage of the surveillance system failure."

"The rebels?" Emma asked.

"Slaves and crew members with the guts to rebel against Del Conte."

Cole nodded, then whispered, "I'm going to circle around in back of the guy."

Emma grabbed his arm. "Too dangerous!"

"You've got a better idea?"

Emma took a breath to steady herself. "Let me catch his attention. I'll tell him the two of you have left the room, and I don't want to get shot. He won't necessarily believe it, but he'll listen to me, and it will give you time to get into a better position."

Cole hated her putting herself in danger. The guard could shoot first and ask questions later, but it sounded like their best chance to get the drop on the guy.

"Stay down,"

"I will."

Emma looked around, found a cloth napkin lying on the deck and attached it to a wooden stick that still held a deflated balloon dangling from one end. She pulled off the shrunken blue piece of rubber and thrust the white flag carefully into the air. Immediately bullets shredded the fabric.

"Don't," she called out. "I'm alone and scared."

"Alone?"

"The two guys ran off."

The guard made a scoffing sound. "Like I believe that. Show yourself."

"So you can shoot me?"

As she spoke, she watched both Cole and Walker snaking across the floor, moving on elbows and stomachs, heading for the back of the bar.

"Help me out. Where is everyone?" she called, only half her mind focused on the conversation as she saw Cole exposed to the shooter for a few seconds. When he made it to cover again, she let out the breath she'd been holding.

Please, God, don't let anything happen to him, she prayed.

In the brig, he had scared the shit out of her by changing into a wolf. She wouldn't have believed it if she hadn't seen it with her own eyes. Or would she?

She'd been attracted to Cole since the moment they'd met, and she knew the feeling was mutual, yet at the same time she'd known there was something different about him. And known that he was fighting his attraction to her. Now he said she was his mate.

Like hell. Unless she wanted to be.

"You think I'm going to trust you?" the man behind the bar shouted, and she realized how dangerous it was to let her mind wander when they were under attack.

"I could say the same thing. You work for Del Conte," she answered.

"I'm just doing my job."

"You happy with the job?"

"The pay is good."

"But the assignments are crap, right?"

Before he could answer, she heard a muffled cry. Since her view was blocked, and she couldn't be sure what was going on, her heart leaped into her throat.

She ached to dash to Cole's aid. That was too dangerous, but she couldn't even shout to him, not without giving something away. With no other choice, she sat where she was with her bottom lip between her teeth, praying that the plan had worked.

Finally, Cole called out. "All clear."

When he stood up, she breathed out a sigh of relief.

"We'd better get out of here," Ben advised.

"With Karen," Emma reminded him.

"Hopefully." They followed him across the room to another one of the doors that were hidden in the walls.

Beyond was another hallway that led to an interior room. At one side were cages.

Karen, still wearing the sheer white kimono, stood in one of the enclosures, her hands clasping the bars. When she saw Ben, she shrank back. "Please," she gasped. "Don't hurt me."

"We're here to get you off the ship," Emma answered.

The girl's gaze swung to her. "It is you!"

"You know me?"

"From school. Didn't you go to the Carlton Academy?"

"Yes. Did somebody ask you about me?"

"Yes. A woman came in here late last night and showed me pictures of the two of you. She wanted to know if I'd seen you before."

"What did you say?"

"That I saw you come through the Tropical Lounge." She turned to Emma. "And that maybe you went to school with me. I'm sorry. I guess I shouldn't have mentioned that."

"It's all right," Emma answered automatically, thinking that Karen had unwittingly blown her cover. But that didn't matter now. She continued, "We're on the ship because your father hired us."

Cole spoke. "You already know Emma, and I'm Cole Marshall. We work for Decorah Security."

"Why didn't you get me out when I saw you?"

"Because we were under guard," Cole answered. "Now we've broken out of the brig, and we have to get you off the ship."

It was then that Emma remembered something that had slipped her mind in the past few frantic hours. She fought not to look sick. "We were supposed to call the rescue ship with the transmitter in my purse. In the lipstick. But I don't have it with me."

"We'll have to make alternate arrangements," Cole bit out, then looked at Ben. "I assume Del Conte has an escape boat."

"Yes."

"Can we get to it?"

"If we're lucky." While he stepped to the barred door and pushed in a code, Emma turned to the lockers and began opening doors. She found a blue uniform shirt and pants, which she pulled out.

As soon as the cell door was open, Karen charged out, looking relieved but also worried.

"Turn around," Emma said to the two men. When they complied, she stepping forward and handed the clothing to Karen. The girl glanced at the men's backs, then stepped into the pants under her kimono skirt. When she had them on, Emma pulled off the gown and Karen slipped into the shirt before reaching to roll up the pants legs and sleeves.

She looked at Emma. "Are we really getting out of here?"

"Yes," she answered with more confidence than she felt.

There were more weapons in racks in the holding area. They each took a spare. And extra ammunition.

"Where's the escape boat?" Cole asked Walker.

"In a docking area on Deck Two. He can flood the whole compartment and open doors to the sea."

Emma thought about that.

"What if Del Conte floods the compartment, and we can't get the doors open? We'll drown."

"Let's assume we can," Cole bit out.

Emma nodded. Without the signal device, their only other alternative was to jump off the ship and swim or try for one of the lifeboats. Both of which would leave them sitting ducks.

Walker looked at Cole and Emma. "Both of you, put on the rest of the uniforms. You might pass for security.

They riffled through more lockers and both found uniform shirts. Cole also found shoes that were only a size too small. Emma had a choice between Bozo the Clown and barefoot. She chose the latter.

The security chief gave them a critical look. "You'll pass," he said to Cole. "But you look like a kid in her dad's uniform," he told Emma.

"Thanks."

He led the way down the corridor again. Emma was next, followed by Karen. Cole brought up the rear, and she hated leaving him in that position, but it made sense.

When more footsteps sounded in the corridor, Emma clenched her hand on the automatic weapon she was holding.

"We don't know how many they are," Walker whispered. "Duck in here." He opened a door, and they stepped into a room that felt like it was freezing. Only a dim light hung from the ceiling, giving Emma a view of large drawers along one wall and a metal table in front of them.

"The morgue?" she asked Walker.

"Yeah." His voice was gritty.

She gave him a direct look. "You don't like this place."

"I've spent too much time here."

"Because Del Conte is rough on his staff?"

"Something like that," he clipped out, telling her that he didn't want to discuss it.

Walker locked the door from the inside. When footsteps paused outside their hiding place, Emma tensed. Whoever was out there tried the door, then moved on.

She sagged against the wall, trying not to breathe in the odor of death.

Turning to Walker she said, "Someone was killed in the hallway when we first arrived, weren't they?"

"Yes."

"Who?"

"A slave who was trying to get off the ship when the hovercraft arrived."

"And you lied about it."

"Of course. You think I had a choice if I wanted to maintain my cover?" he asked in a hard voice. "Just like I

171

had to interrogate Cole last night when Stella called me. Lucky she reached me and not Greg. Otherwise, Cole would probably be dead."

Emma winced.

Cole took her arm. "Let's not get off track. We have to get off the *Windward*. After unlocking the door, he cautiously opened it a crack. No one was outside.

Walker led them to the stairs. They were on their way down when the third floor landing opened.

A tall, blond woman stepped out. Allison from the beauty salon. She was followed by Anna, the other beautician.

Allison eyes widened as she stared at the guns. "Don't shoot me. What's going on?"

Emma started to answer, but stopped abruptly when Walker shook his head.

"What's going on with you?" he asked.

"Something's happening. I heard gunfire. I'm scared. Is there any chance of getting off the ship?"

"No," Walker snapped."

"Then where are you going?" Allison asked.

Walker's gaze flicked from Allison to Anna and back again. Apparently he didn't trust the blond woman.

Allison's speculative gaze swept over them and fixed on Karen. 'What's *she* doing with you?"

While Emma was considering the answer, Anna took a quick step back just as Allison brought a gun from the folds of her black smock.

"All of you, drop your weapons."

As she spoke, a shot reverberated off the walls of the stairwell.

CHAPTER SIXTEEN

While Emma watched in shock, Allison slid to the floor, a red stain spreading out beneath her.

Anna was standing behind her, a gun in her hand.

Walker turned to the others. "Anna's one of the leaders of the rebels. I've been meeting with her in secret—when I could."

"And Allison's been spying on me for months," Anna added. "When the surveillance system went down, I left the salon, but Allison tagged along. She stuck to me like glue. I had to pretend I was scared of the mutiny, but I was hoping I could hook up with you."

Walker nodded.

"I was pretty sure this had something to do with Karen." She looked at Emma. "After the way you reacted when you saw that hair on the floor."

"I guess I should have been more subtle."

"No. I'm trained to be observant." She turned to Walker. "You know there are others desperate to get off the boat."

"We can't take a crowd. We'll have to come back for them," he said, then gave her a sharp look. "I guess you'd better tell me how you knew where to find us."

She raised her chin. "I planted a tracker on Karen. It's also a transmitter."

The girl gasped. "Where?"

"In your butterfly hair ornament. Remember, I told you not to take it off."

"Lucky I didn't," she murmured.

"How many people are opposing Del Conte?" Cole asked Anna.

"I don't know exactly," she answered. "Some slaves recruit others—cautiously. We're in—how do you call it?—cells." She looked at Cole and Emma. "One of us was killed when you arrived."

"Ben told us. I'm so sorry," Emma murmured.

"Not your fault. He was taking too much of a chance. There was no way he was going to board that hovercraft."

"We'd better get going," Walker broke in. "Come on."

They started down the stairs again, all keeping their eyes on the next doorway. But they passed it without incident and proceeded to Deck Two where the escape boat was located.

"There will be guards," Walker said as they hurried along a hallway. "I'll go in first and assess the situation."

"And then what?" Emma asked.

"Maybe I can convince them I'm still working with Del Conte."

Ben Walker moved to the front and pressed his thumb against a pad beside the hatch

When it opened, he took a deep breath and let it out before striding inside like he had every right to be there.

He stayed in the doorway as he looked around to see five of Del Conte's most loyal guards stationed around the area. They were all hardened security men. All of them enjoyed working on the *Windward.* Lording it over the slaves and sometimes participating in rough scenes. He knew that two of these guys had been responsible for the deaths of three cast members.

"Chief!" one of them called out. "We've been trying to reach you, but the comms system is down. We got a hand-delivered message that the *Windward* is under attack," one of the men called out.

"Is it the rebels?" another asked.

"It's Cole Mason and Emma Ray who came on board yesterday."

"All by themselves?"

"Some of the rebels have joined them," Walker conceded. He wished he'd had more time to think of a story before stepping through the door. "I've got everything under control," he went on. "The master is coming down, just as soon as he's sure the area's safe. I want you outside the hatch in case there's trouble."

The men were tense but compliant as they moved toward the door. Ben was starting to think that he'd pulled this off when a voice called out,

"Wait a minute."

Greg stepped from behind a stack of supply cartons.

"Don't listen to the bastard. He's helping Mason and Ray," Greg shouted.

Before anyone could fire, Ben ducked back out the hatch, slamming it behind him.

Karen screamed as a hail of bullets hit the metal but didn't penetrate.

"It was working," Walker growled. "Until Greg showed up. He's been desperate to get something on me that he could take to Del Conte—and get my job."

"Now what?" Cole asked in a grating voice.

Walker stepped closer to them, his voice low. "There's a hatch in the ceiling. I can get in, but I'm going to need a diversion."

"I can do it," Cole answered.

Emma looked from him to Walker and back again.

"But you don't have any way to communicate, once you're out of sight," she said. "Cole won't know when to start the diversion."

"Yeah," Walker acknowledged, trying to think of a way around the problem.

Anna provided the answer by pulling the butterfly clip out of Karen's hair and clicking her thumbnail against it. The sound echoed in her watch.

"You do have a way to communicate," she said. "The transmitter."

She handed the butterfly to Walker. "Take it with you. Signal when you're in position," she said.

He took the ornament, turning it in his hand, then slipping it into his pocket. "Thanks."

"How long before you can open the hatch?" Cole asked.

"Five minutes, if I'm lucky."

"Do the men in there know about it?" Emma asked.

"That's the luck part."

Anna gripped his arm. "Be careful."

"I will," he said before heading back the way they'd come.

Ben took a side corridor, then ducked into one of Del Conte's secret passages. The man had had them built at strategic locations around the ship. He used them to prowl around without being seen and as alternate routes to secure locations. Nobody was supposed to know about them, but Ben had discovered their existence when he'd been poking around in the master's computer system. He snorted. Only a megalomaniac would call himself "The Master," but Del Conte definitely qualified.

At the entrance to a hatch, he stopped and listened, then cautiously opened the metal door and stepped inside where he found a ladder of rungs attached to the wall.

As he started to climb, he reflected that he could get himself killed on this mission, but that wouldn't be anything new. A couple of years ago he'd gotten into a nasty situation that had left him technically dead for five minutes. A long time, when you considered what oxygen deprivation did to the brain.

He knew what it had done to him. Given him an unusual ability that had changed his life. He didn't talk about it to anyone. But he'd used it a time or two, especially after he'd taken on the covert mission on the *Windward*.

At the top of the ladder he paused to inspect the hatch in front of him. Then, working as quietly as possible, he turned the handle that opened the cover.

Everyone's tension grew as the minutes ticked by and there was no communication with the security chief.

"Did something happen?" Karen whispered. "I mean, what if he met more guards."

"Let's hope he's still on track," Emma answered, thinking that if he was out of commission, they'd have to go to plan B—whatever that was.

Finally they heard the flicking sound coming from the watch.

"Thank God," Emma murmured.

"Get back," Cole said in a gritty voice. Emma gave him a long look, but she couldn't come up with an alternative to his drawing the guards' fire.

The women moved a few yards down the hall and into an alcove, with Anna facing in one direction and Emma in the other, each ready to fire if they saw someone coming.

Cole moved to the hatch and turned the lever, opening the door a crack. It creaked, drawing instant fire from the men inside the docking area. Bullets hit the door and bounced back.

Cole slammed the door and waited thirty seconds. When he opened it again, there was another burst of fire, but this time it wasn't directed toward the door. The shots were going in the other direction.

Then silence.

After long tense moments, the watch began making the flicking sound again.

"He's in," Cole called out. As he reached for the door handle, Emma wanted to grab him, but she knew they couldn't stay in the hallway forever.

As he disappeared inside, she felt her heart start to pound. She'd been shaken by the wolf, but the shock was over. What if something happened to him now?

The thought of going on without him made a wave of cold sweep over her. She'd just found out what they meant to each other and she ached to explore the bond she felt between them.

Her attention zinged back to the hallway when she heard stealthy footsteps advancing down the corridor. Somebody had heard the gunfire and knew the escape boat was under attack.

She and Anna exchanged glances. Anna nodded. Both of them stepped in front of Karen, faced in the direction of the sound. Emma risked a glance around the corner and saw two guards come cautiously down the corridor, machine guns at the ready. One was a tall, dark-haired woman.

Emma and Anna had never worked together before, but they had to do it now.

"I'll take the woman," Emma whispered.

Anna nodded.

Emma's heart was pounding as she waited for the attackers to come closer.

"Now," Anna whispered.

They both darted out, taking the assault team by surprise. Emma had never shot a woman, but she knew her life depended on doing it now.

As they fired, Cole charged back out the door, his face alarmed and his gun raised. But the guards were already lying unmoving in a pool of blood on the floor.

"Holy shit," he whispered as he saw the woman lying on the ground. "It's Stella."

"The bitch who interrogated you last night?"

"I guess she won't be doing it to anyone else."

"There could be more on the way," Anna said. "We'd better get out of here."

Emma followed Cole through the hatch. She gasped when she saw five dead guards strewn around the metal deck. One of them was Greg, who'd first served them drinks on the hovercraft. A thousand years ago.

Walker stepped out from behind a pile of containers. Relief flooded through her, until she saw blood spreading on the arm of his uniform shirt.

"Not an artery," he said in a matter-of-fact voice as he took in her worried expression. "Everybody inside."

Emma stepped back through the door, motioning to Anna and Karen who hurried to join her and the men.

"They know I'd try for the dock. Reinforcements will be coming," Walker said as he slammed the door, then sent a spray of bullets into the control mechanism.

"I guess it's either the outer door or nothing," Cole said.

It was wet and clammy inside the sea dock, making Emma shiver as she looked around. They were in a large open area, nothing like the passenger sections of the ship. The walls of the chamber were metal, with metal catwalks around three sides of a rectangular pool of seawater in the middle of which floated a sleek speedboat. Emma saw why they couldn't take everybody who wanted to leave the *Windward*. There was room for maybe six people, if they arranged themselves like Vienna sausages in a can.

Walker strode to another control panel and pressed a row of switches.

"Shit."

"What?" Cole asked.

"The sea doors won't open."

"That's right." The observation came from a television mounted high on the wall.

Emma gasped when she saw that Bruno Del Conte was looking down on them, a satisfied expression on his handsome face.

Bruno Del Conte's anger flared as he looked down on the bastards who had locked themselves in the sea dock.

He'd left loyal men in there, but it looked like Walker and Mason had finished them off.

They thought they were in the clear, but they were sadly mistaken. He'd drown them, then escape from the *Windward*, and activate the explosive charges to blow up the ship when he was far enough away.

Contemplating the destruction gave him a few moment's satisfaction—until he focused on Ben Walker again.

What the hell was he doing with Mason and Ray? Were they paying him to help them? Or was it something personal, something that Bruno didn't know.

He studied the group again. It included that Asian woman from the beauty salon. And Karen Hopewell.

Had Mason and Ray come here to rescue her? Had that been their mission all along? And he hadn't realized it.

Walker should have figured that out.

No. Forget Walker. He'd only been stalling while he played his own game.

Bruno had trusted his security chief. Relied on him. And look what had happened. Well, never again. He'd use security men in the future, but he'd never confide in them again.

That was for later. When he'd had time to regroup. For now, he had to clear his escape route. His mind considered contingencies. Maybe he didn't have to wait for them to drown. Maybe there was a quicker way.

He'd had the ship modified to his specifications. Now he took a narrow passage downward which would give him closer access to the interior dock. For now, he had to keep them busy.

"Did you really think you could get away so easily?" he asked. "You're all going to drown in there, like the rats you are."

Emma's chest tightened as she heard a clanking noise and saw the water level in the pool begin to rise. The *Windward*'s owner must be in the control room, and he was flooding the compartment. She looked up, seeing the metal ceiling above them. When the water rose to that level, there would be no more air to breathe in here.

"Maybe not." Cole raised his Uzi and shot the television screen, shattering Del Conte's view of the dock. At least he wasn't going to see them drown.

The water was lapping at the top of the catwalk as Walker and Cole conferred.

Cole turned to Emma. "You can handle the boat's controls, right?"

"Yes."

"Then get the women into the craft and start the engine."

Emma looked from the women to the boat and back again. They could ride the water level up. But then what? Trusting that Cole and Ben had a plan, she pulled on one of the mooring lines, guiding the boat to the metal walkway where water now sloshed.

The two other women scrambled in. Emma followed and examined the controls. The key was in the ignition, and she turned it, holding her breath until the engine caught.

She could see the two men moving along the catwalk, sloshing through water. How long before the whole enclosure filled up?

"Do you think Del Conte can hear us?" Cole asked.

"Don't know," Walker answered. "Maybe it doesn't matter."

From the other side of the locked door, they could hear hammering.

"Guys trying to get in?"

"Sounds like it."

The hammering was replaced by a spray of gunfire. But Del Conte had designed the room so that entry wasn't going to be easy.

"Won't the guards out there get slammed against the wall by a big wave if they break through."

"Their problem."

Cole looked from the hatch to the outer bay door. "I take it we can't shoot through there either."

"The metal's bulletproof. You might be able to shoot out the windows." He pointed to high, narrow panes that let in slivers of light. Unfortunately, not enough water can get out of those to do us any good. But there's an alternative." Walker gestured toward a ladder in one corner of the enclosure. Lowering his voice, he continued, "Tricky Bruno has a lot of contingency plans. They weren't for public consumption, but I was able to break into his computer files and poke around. There are plastic explosives up there we can use to break out."

"Yeah, I guess he can get anything he wants. What else does he have up his sleeve?"

"He's got charges set that can blow up the whole ship if he wants."

"Christ."

"If he's got the nerve to do it."

"Maybe he still thinks he can get away."

Walker sloshed to the ladder and began to climb, wincing as he used his bad arm.

Cole followed, looking back to see Emma watching intently. If he didn't get her out of here, he was going to kill Frank Decorah. Except that he couldn't because he and Emma would be dead.

Above him, Walker opened a compartment and handed down a packet to Cole. He took it and started for the catwalk. There was already two feet of water on the deck, making it hard to walk.

He'd had some experience with explosive charges, but then he'd been trying to break in somewhere. Now he was racing against time—to get out of this death trap.

Walker joined him, and they conferred at the metal doors, deciding where to set the charges, well at the sides.

Looking back he saw that the boat was rising toward the ceiling. If they didn't blow the doors soon, it was all over.

He and Walker each took a packet of plastic explosives and molded them against the door, then set the detonators and turned back to the escape boat.

They had to swim for it now, Walker awkwardly with one arm disabled. But the two women in the back helped haul them in.

"How long? Emma asked.

"Three minutes. Already counting." A lifetime, under the circumstances. Was the water rising faster, or was that his imagination. And was he imagining that the air was getting harder to breathe?

Raising the Uzi, he shot some holes in the glass panels of the metal door, hoping that would help the oxygen situation.

"Get down," he told the women, moving to shield Emma from the blast.

A clanking in the ceiling made him look up toward a hatch he hadn't seen before.

More rasping followed, and he tensed as a metal plate slid to the side, then dropped into the water with a splash.

The women in the back of the boat screamed as a grinning Del Conte loomed directly above them, an AK47 in his hand.

"Got ya!"

CHAPTER SEVENTEEN

Del Conte was so focused on his tricky move that he didn't realize his fatal mistake. His grin faded when he realized how close the boat was to the hatch.

As the ship owner began to fire on the people below, Cole surged upward, grabbing the barrel of the gun and giving a mighty yank.

Del Conte stopped shooting and switched his effort to stopping himself from tumbling through the hatch. Maybe if he'd let go of the gun, he could have backed up, but he kept up the tug of war with Cole, who had the greater strength and the advantage of gravity. The ship's owner lost his footing, tumbling downward through the hatch and into the boat, still clutching the gun.

He and Cole were struggling for the weapon when Karen surged forward, a metal first aid box in her hand. She crashed it down on Del Conte's head, and the man went limp. Then she kept hitting. Raising and lowering the box, turning the side of his head into a bloody pulp.

"Enough," Emma called, staring at the young woman.

As Karen stood in stunned shock, Walker and Anna pitched the *Windward*'s owner out of the boat.

"Thank God," Anna wheezed, seconds before a tremendous boom filled the confined space. As it blew the doors off the dock area, it knocked the passengers off their feet and they fell together in a heap in the bottom of the boat. All but Emma who was holding tight to the wheel.

"Hang on," she screamed as she struggled to keep the craft steady while a wave of water surged toward them, slamming them against the back wall, then propelling them forward toward the ragged hole where the doors had been.

Del Conte's limp body shot past, disappearing below the surface of the churning water.

"Duck," Emma shouted, scrunching down to avoid a jagged piece of metal hanging down in the doorway.

As they rocketed out into the open sea, Cole felt a surge of relief, until he saw the water seeping into the bottom of the boat. He'd been too busy to notice earlier that Del Conte's bullets had pierced the bottom of the craft.

He emptied the first aid kit, using the box to bail water. The women had also found containers holding emergency supplies and were frantically scooping out water.

"What about the radio?" he asked Walker.

The security chief pointed to the cockpit.

"Take over the bailing," Cole said as he maneuvered to the front and clicked on the communications equipment.

They'd left Florida with an automatic system. Now he began broadcasting on a public frequency. With Del Conte out of the way, there was no need to speak on a private channel or in code.

"This is Cole Marshall. Cole Marshall. And Emma Richards. We have cleared the *Windward*. We have KH with us. We are in a sinking boat and need immediate assistance." Using the GPS in the cockpit, he gave their coordinates.

At first he heard nothing, and he thought he hadn't gotten through. Behind him, Walker and the women were losing the battle to keep the craft afloat.

He kept repeating the message, wondering if he should broadcast a general May Day message.

Finally, the speaker crackled. "Cole Marshall, this is Decorah Security. We have your location. We will rendezvous momentarily."

"Over there," Emma shouted, pointing toward the right as a cabin cruiser came speeding toward them.

When it pulled alongside, Cole helped Karen to the ladder, guiding her up.

"Go," he said to Emma as soon as Karen was on board the rescue craft. She scrambled up, followed by Anna, then Walker. Cole was last, watching water swamp the speedboat.

"Get up here, you fool," Frank Decorah called, obviously unable to keep his cool.

"Aye, aye, sir," Cole answered as he complied.

On board, he stepped into the cabin and saw Karen holding tight to an older man. Her father!

Apparently Morton Hopewell had insisted on joining the rescue party. Cole shuddered. What if they hadn't been able to free Karen?

"I am so sorry this happened to you," Hopewell was saying. You're 're sure you're all right?"

"Yes." She looked back at the group who had come aboard. "Thanks to Emma and Cole and the others. Ben Walker was Del Conte's security chief."

The older Hopewell reared back. "Then what the hell is he doing here?"

"He was working under cover," Anna said.

"And you are?" Hopewell demanded.

"On the staff in the beauty salon," the Asian woman supplied. "I was part of a group trying to take Del Conte down.

Where is Del Conte?" Hopewell asked.

Cole glanced at Karen, figuring she could fill her dad in on the details if she wanted to. "Drowned. He won't threaten you or anyone else again."

"But there are more people who need to be rescued from the *Windward*," Anna said. "Cast members who are in danger from the security staff."

"Cast members? That's what he calls them—like at Disney World."

"Yes."

"We have a team standing by," Decorah answered. He turned to Walker. "How would you suggest we go in?"

"Broadcast to the ship that Del Conte is dead. Anyone who wants to get off will be given passage to the mainland."

"Some of the guards are dangerous," Anna breathed.

"But a lot of them are good men who got trapped here just the way you did," Ben said. "I can give you a list of the ones with criminal records. You can have the Miami police standing by to take care of those."

"Good idea," Frank answered, then turned to Emma and Cole. "Excellent job."

"Thanks," Cole answered, thinking that they almost hadn't made it. But he'd save that until later.

"Let's go where we can talk." Frank ushered Emma and Cole into a private cabin.

As soon as the door was closed, Cole rounded on Decorah. "That was an unacceptable risk. Emma and I could have gotten killed."

Frank's expression turned apologetic. "I know that now. I didn't know it when I sent you. And I was desperate to get Karen back."

"What's she to you?"

He swallowed. "My daughter."

"What?" Emma breathed.

"She doesn't know it. And don't tell her."

"Then what's she doing with Hopewell?" Cole asked.

Sadness suffused Frank's features. "Her mother died when she was born. And I was dealing with a missing leg. I couldn't take care of her on my own. Morton and Sarah Hopewell were desperate to adopt a child. When they told me they'd love her like their own, I knew giving her to them was the right thing to do."

He dragged in a breath and let it out. "She's been happy with them. They gave her more than I ever could."

Cole nodded, understanding why his boss had seemed so personally involved in the rescue mission.

"That's why her face looked familiar to us?"

"Yes. And she has her mother's red hair. But that's the end of this discussion. Give me the executive summary of the mission, so I can feel guilty about putting you in so much danger."

"It turned out okay," Cole answered.

He and Emma supplied a brief account of their time on the *Windward*.

"I've got that recorded, but I'll need a detailed written report," Decorah said when they were finished, all business again.

Emma ran a hand through her hair, obviously still coping with what they'd learned a few minutes ago. "Did you bring clothes for us?"

"As a matter of fact, I did. And you can shower, too."

He handed them each a suitcase, and they disappeared into separate cabins to shower and change.

Cole was glad to wash off the sordid atmosphere of the *Windward*. When he'd dried off, he chose jeans and a dark knit shirt. When Emma came out, she was wearing chinos and a white camp shirt, a look which was much better suited to her than the outfits she'd been forced to wear on the *Windward*.

When they joined the group in the ship's lounge, Frank was talking earnestly to Ben Walker, who was relaxing in an easy chair, his arm bandaged.

The conversation broke off when Cole and Emma reappeared, and he wondered what they'd been talking about.

"I could use a drink," Frank said.

He looked at Cole. "Maybe you want double strength herbal tea."

"Yeah," Cole answered and glanced at Emma.

"Tea will do," she said.

"You've adopted Cole's habits," their boss said with a speculative look at them.

"Maybe," Emma snapped. Frank took the hint and left her staring out the window toward the mainland.

Cole tried to get comfortable in a leather chair. But he was too tense. He ached for some privacy with Emma, but at the same time he was dreading the conversation they were going to have when they were alone.

He got a reprieve when the boat docked, and Karen and her father came up to them.

"We're both very grateful for what you did," Hopewell said.

"We were doing our jobs."

"At great risk to yourselves. I'd like to reward you for that."

"No need," Cole said brusquely.

"I didn't mean to offend," Hopewell answered.

"You didn't," Emma said quickly. "We were both thankful everything worked out."

Karen looked at her. "We weren't friends in school, but I'm so grateful to you now. If I ever want to talk to you, is that all right?"

"Of course." She held out her arms, and Karen came into them. No, they hadn't been friends, but they'd shared an experience that bonded them together. And Emma knew that it had helped mature both of them. They hugged, before Emma eased away. "Take care," she murmured.

"I will. Thanks to you. I guess I have some thinking to do—about my life."

"Don't make any decisions until you have a chance to decompress."

"I won't."

Cole shook hands with Hopewell, and they left the ship, rolling the suitcases Decorah had brought them.

The Infinity was where he had parked it, but he realized he was missing his wallet and keys.

Decorah must have known there would be a problem because he handed Cole and Emma wallets with ID and credit cards—plus another set of car keys for Cole.

"You turned down Hopewell, but don't turn down the bonus I'm giving you," he said. "For getting someone important to me out of there."

"I'd say we earned it," Cole replied.

"And you two are due for some R&R. You have a suite reserved at the St. Augustine," he added, mentioning a luxury resort in the area. I'll expect you back in two weeks."

"Thanks," Cole answered, then cleared his throat. "I get the feeling you're going to offer Ben Walker a job."

"Do you approve?"

"Yes," both Cole and Emma answered.

"That's an excellent recommendation."

"Go on. Get out of here and try to relax," Frank said.

Cole wasn't going to ask why their boss assumed they were going off together, and apparently Emma didn't want to question it, either.

He counted it as a good sign that she hadn't said she wanted to go back to DC immediately—alone.

"Are we going to talk?" he asked.

"Eventually," she snapped.

They had been driving for ten minutes, when she pointed to a strip mall and said, "Stop at that shopping center."

The tone of her voice made him wonder what she needed. It also made him think that he'd better not ask.

He found a parking place, and she got out. "I'll be back in a while," she said, as she marched off.

He sat behind the wheel, waiting for her, his tension growing as the minutes ticked by. Finally, after half an hour, she reappeared holding a small carry bag.

"Did you buy some more clothes?" he asked.

"Some other stuff I needed," she answered. "Let's go to that resort."

The look in her eye didn't reassure him, but at least she was still with him.

He drove to the St. Augustine, where they checked in and were shown to a waterfront suite with a living room, small kitchen, two bedrooms and two marble bathrooms. Maybe Frank hadn't been so sure if they wanted to be together after all.

When Cole had tipped the bellman and closed the door, he turned to Emma.

His stomach was tied in knots, but he struggled to speak normally. "Well, you're still here."

She answered with a little shrug, then folded her arms across her chest.

"Are you afraid of me?"

"Not afraid."

"Then what?"

"You sprang a couple of nasty surprises on me."

"I'm sorry. I didn't have any choices. I couldn't tell you about the incident with the guard. Or about my heritage. Not when microphones could pick up what I said."

"The incident with the guard! You killed him."

"Like you killed Stella in the hall outside the docking area."

She sighed. "Right." After a little hesitation, she asked, "Who killed the guard? You or the wolf?"

"I am the wolf."

"And which one was it last night?"

"The wolf. I woke up in a stateroom—as a wolf. I didn't remember getting that way. Then the guy came in with a gun, and I reacted."

"And then what?"

"I changed back to human form, wrapped him in the bedspread and managed to carry him up a flight of stairs to the next deck, where I dumped him overboard. Do you need to know anything else about it?"

"No. And we're getting away from what I wanted to talk about here."

He wanted to say that the direction of the conversation wasn't his fault, but he figured that pointing it out was a bad idea.

She kept her gaze fixed on him. "Before we went to the *Windward,* you said that you had to be the dominant member of our pretend relationship."

"What about it?" he answered, not liking where this was leading.

"What about our real relationship?"

"What are you asking, exactly?"

"If we're going to . . . stay together, I have to know that there's complete trust between us."

"I trust you."

"I don't think I can take your word for that."

"I was willing to die to protect you."

He saw her swallow. "That was when we were in bad trouble."

"I love you. Nothing's changed. For me."

"You're going to have to prove that."

"How?"

"By doing what you said you couldn't do. Putting yourself in my power."

He knew she was trying to come across as bold when she raised her chin and said. "Let me set up another little game for us to play. Where I'm in total charge of your body."

He tipped his head to one side, as he considered the implications. "As in . . . uh . . . bondage?"

"Damn straight."

"What . . . uh . . . do you have in mind?"

She stiffened her posture and made her voice authoritative. "If I spell it out, then doing it won't mean anything."

"So you want to test me?"

"Yes."

He didn't like it. Ever since he'd left his home pack—his father's pack—he'd been the alpha wolf in his own domain. That meant something to him, but he understood where she was coming from. And he also understood that she was his mate, and the idea of living without her was too painful to contemplate. Which left him no choice but to do what she asked.

His mouth was so dry he could hardly speak, but he managed to say, "Let's get it over with."

"Okay, then. I want you naked on your back on that bed. With your arms spread-eagled. I'm going to tie you down, and I expect you to stay that way, until I release you."

Well, that would certainly be a demonstration of trust.

She picked up the bag with the items she'd bought and marched past him into one of the bedrooms where she yanked off the spread and top sheet.

Whirling back to him, she said, "Either take off your clothes, and lie down. Or walk out the door if you want it to be over between us.

CHAPTER EIGHTEEN

"No," Cole whispered.

"No, what?"

"I'm not leaving. I'll do whatever it takes to prove I love you."

He knew she was holding her breath, and when he pulled off his shirt, she let the air out of her lungs.

When he tossed his shirt onto the chair, he could see her sweeping her gaze over his broad chest. She kept up the scrutiny as he kicked off his shoes, then removed his jeans and briefs.

He wished this game of hers wasn't arousing him, but there was no way to hide the erection that was now standing out from his body.

She didn't comment on that, but she made her voice commanding, apparently in keeping with the role she had set herself to play.

"Lie down."

He did as she asked.

"Spread your arms and legs."

He did that, too, watching as she pulled four brightly colored scarves from the bag she'd set on the floor. Quickly she tied them to the straps on the side of the mattress.

Probably he could have pulled himself loose, but he let her have her way, even when he couldn't stop the pounding of his heart.

As he lay in that totally vulnerable position, waiting to find out what would happen next, she took a step back and began to unbutton her shirt. Decorah Security must have packed some sexy underwear in her bag, because she was wearing a peach colored bra that didn't do much to hide her breasts.

Next she took off her slacks, revealing her matching panties.

Standing beside the bed, she looked down at him and reached behind her back to unhook her bra. Her beautiful breasts sprang free, so close to him he could touch them, if he weren't tied down.

Languidly, she lifted them as though she were offering them to him, watching his face as she did.

When his breath caught, she reached down and lightly stroked her finger along the length of his rock-hard cock, giving him a jolt of sensation.

Had she gotten the idea from the Mayan ceremony? He wasn't going to ask. At least not yet.

As he watched, she took out one more scarf, with black and white flowers. When she folded it into a long strip, laid it over his eyes and tied it at the side of his head, he felt another jolt—this time of alarm.

"What are you doing?"

"I think it's obvious. Can you see?"

"No."

"Good. And I don't want you to speak again until I give you permission. Nod if you agree."

He nodded and pressed his lips together, hating this. Well, hating it but turned on, too. He'd never imagined Emma Richards doing anything like this. And never imagined himself in this situation, either.

"Nice. Very nice," she murmured. "Do you know, you look very sexy like that."

If she could have seen his eyes, she would have known he was glaring in the direction of her voice.

"I think I know what you'd like me to do, but you're going to have to wait for that," she murmured, as she sat down on the side of the bed, stroking his shoulders, combing her fingers through the hair on his chest before finding his nipples, squeezing and pulling on them until he couldn't hold back a moan.

Her hands drifted lower, over his ribs, down his body, sliding over his thighs, avoiding his aching cock.

He was in an agony of need, and if he hadn't agreed to her game, he would have ripped his hands free of the scarves and grabbed her.

The priests at the Mayan ceremony had used feathers on the woman. Apparently she had those, too, because he felt their tickle against his ribs, then his belly, then his cock.

"It's a cat toy," she said, unable to keep a little chuckle out of her voice as she tickled under his arms, on the bottoms of his feet, then back and forth against his penis again.

His hips bucked, telling her he needed more.

But she ignored the entreaty.

"You're very aroused, aren't you," she murmured. "You don't have to answer that. I can tell," she said, as she touched the drop of moisture at the end of his cock, then rubbed onto the head.

He couldn't hold back a groan.

When she stroked her finger lightly up and down his shaft, he wanted to beg her to grasp him in her hand. But she only kept up the maddening stroking before reaching lower and fondling his balls.

Again he groaned.

"I could straddle you," she murmured. "I know you'd like to be inside me now. This is turning me on, too. I'm all wet and slippery. All ready for you."

He made a pleading sound.

"Maybe later."

She went away, and he bit his lip to keep from calling her back. He could hear her riffling through the bag she'd brought and wondered what new torture she was planning.

"You need to be punished for the way you lied to me."

Punished, how?

He heard a sound not unlike a whip cracking before something came flying down on his shoulder. Only the business end was broader than a whip. And shorter.

As he tried to figure out what it was, he almost laughed. Jesus, it must be a fly swatter.

Laughter fled when she whipped his shoulders and chest hard enough to sting, but he took it in silence.

When she went to lighter swats on his cock, the little stinging blows only increased his arousal.

She stopped abruptly, and he wondered what torture she was going to perpetrate next. Not being able to see was the worst part. But obviously she'd planned it that way.

The mattress shifted and he felt her come down beside him on the bed.

In the next moment, something cold and sharp poked against his neck. A knife.

When she pressed the blade more firmly against his skin, he lay absolutely still, his heart pounding.

After all that, was she going to kill him. Was that her way of getting out of the relationship? If she didn't want to be with him, maybe that was the best thing.

Those thoughts made no sense, not if she really did love him. Still, they went through his mind as he waited with his pulse pounding to find out what she was planning.

When he heard her sob, his heart lurched inside his chest. Would she kill him? Kill them both because the thought of being a werewolf's mate was too much for her to take?

"Oh Lord, Cole," she sobbed out, and he heard the knife bounce onto the rug. "I thought I was being so clever. I thought I could do this to make you understand how much you scared me. To make you *feel* it. Like I did. but I can't. Punishing you is like punishing myself."

Frantically she pulled at the scarf that covered his face, tugging it over his head so that her eyes could meet his.

"Oh, Cole. Cole."

As she took off the blindfold, he ripped at the bindings on his wrists and ankles, easily freeing himself as he reached for her, clasping her to him. She came willingly, then brought her mouth down to his for a frantic kiss.

He held on to her as though his life depended on it, rocking her in his arms, his hands skimming over her back, into her hair, then cupping the back of her head.

She moaned into his mouth, her own arms clasping him tightly as they rocked together on the bed, frantic to get close to each other and closer still.

As they held each other for long moments, he knew what he had hoped was true. She wanted to be his mate.

And he would tell her how much that meant to him, then tell her all the things he had neglected to explain.

But first, he would claim her for his own in a way he hadn't been able to do on the ship. Freely, joyfully, completely.

He eased far enough away so that his hand could drift down her body and dip into the moist heat between her legs. She cried out in pleasure as he parted her most intimate flesh so that he could take a gliding trip from her vagina to her clit, then back again, as he watched her face, drinking in her reaction.

"Oh Cole, Cole. I know I belong to you."

The words thrilled him.

"No more than I belong to you," he answered, fighting to keep his voice from cracking as he spoke. "I want to make you understand how much that means to me."

"Then make love to me. Now."

She reached out, pulling him on top of her and at the same time guiding him inside.

All at once, he was there, feeling the tight caress of her sheath. And his only choice was to move his hips, sending a surge of sensation through both of them.

The intensity of their joining swept over them, their hips rising and falling, creating friction that drove them toward a rocketing climax he had never imagined.

Right here. Right now. The two of them flying into a world of heat and light where their only option was to cling to each other.

This was what he had always longed for, even when he hadn't known it.

The firestorm swept over them, leaving them both limp and breathless.

When they came back to earth, he shifted his side, taking her with him, holding her in his arms.

"I wanted you from the first moment I saw you," he whispered. "I kept fighting it. But eventually, this would have happened. Even without that trip through the dark corridors of the *Windward*."

"The ship made it impossible for us to keep . . . rubbing each other the wrong way."

"I hope you can accept me for what I am."

"I think I have to." She looked up at him, her eyes dark with emotion. "Even when I don't know much about it yet."

"I'll tell you everything. Anything."

"Do you, uh, turn into a wolf when the moon is full?"

He shook his head. "Only when I want to. Forget about all the old myths." He cleared his throat. "In my family, the men go through their first change at puberty." He paused before the next part. "Only about half survive."

"Oh no. That's so sad."

"But my cousin, Ross Marshall, is married to a geneticist who's working on improving the odds."

"What about the girls?"

"It's a sex-linked trait. Until Ross and Megan had a daughter, no girls survived."

"That's . . . just as bad."

"Yeah, it was the family curse for generations. That and the survival rate of the boys. The modern werewolf has advantages over his savage ancestors."

She answered with a little nod.

He cleared his throat. "Around the age of thirty, the Marshall men start looking for a lifemate. I knew it was you almost as soon as we met, only I fought it because I didn't exactly have a rosy family life. But I didn't know how strongly I'd feel about you. When you were in danger on that damn ship, I knew I'd die if anything happened to you."

She kept her gaze steady. "Is that why I feel the same way about you? Because I'm your mate? And some kind of instinct has taken over?"

"My lifemate. Wolves mate for life." He reached for her hand and knit his fingers with hers. "We bonded because of the strong attraction we felt right from the beginning."

It's a compulsion?"

"It's like any two people meeting and falling in love. Only better."

She nodded, but he could see she was still full of questions.

"Does Frank Decorah know about the wolf?"

"Yes."

"How?"

"Six years ago, he found a wounded wolf in the woods, shot by a hunter. He took it home and called a vet who removed the bullet. While the wolf was recovering, he kept it in a cage, but it got an infection and its temperature spiked. While the wolf was feverish, it changed into a man."

200

"That must have been . . . awkward."

He laughed. "It was. But Frank's a guy who rolls with the punches. He accepted me." His gaze turned thoughtful. "Actually, he was like a father to me. Maybe that was because he'd lost Karen, and that left a gap in his life."

Emma nodded.

"Unfortunately, my own father's someone you don't want to spend much time with, but Frank treated me like a son. Before I met him, I was in a dead-end job, working for a wilderness outfitter company. He saw the potential in me. He paid for my college education—and a masters in criminal justice."

"I didn't know."

"Well, that's one reason I'm so loyal to him. The other is that he had more faith in me than I had in myself."

"I understand. But I think he also knew that he'd be getting an outstanding operative. He knew you'd be a fantastic addition to Decorah Security."

"I know that, too. Working for him gave me a focus that I never had before."

She squeezed his hand.

"He knew I'd be right for this assignment. Then I found out he was sending you, and my heart lurched."

"It worked out." She met his gaze. "Because we're an excellent team. He understood that, too. Not just for this assignment."

"I'm thinking he was hoping he could get us together. And he didn't know he was damn near getting us killed."

She settled down beside him, burrowing close.

He held on to her, knowing how lucky he was to have her. They still had problems to iron out. But they would, because they both wanted the relationship to work.

"I used to wonder why you hadn't paired up with anyone," he murmured.

"No one was right for me. Dominant men reminded me of my father. And the nice guys were boring."

"I'm not a nice guy?"

"Nicer than I thought you'd be."

"Thanks. Does that mean you'll marry me?"

"I thought I'd never marry," she murmured. "I thought my life would be all about my job." She turned her head toward him. "Amazing how quickly that changed."

"That's a yes?" he asked, wanting to nail down the answer.

"Yes."

He held her tightly as he asked. "But you want to keep working?"

"Are you going to object to that?"

"I won't stop you. But I'll be biting my claws if you get into anything like the *Windward* assignment again."

"No more than I'll worry about you."

'We don't have to settle everything now," he said. "Just so I know you belong to me—and I belong to you."

"I like it that you included the last part."

He reached for her hand. "There's no other woman I want. There never will be again. Only you. My lifemate."

"Yes."

"We've got time off, and I don't want to waste any of it." He rose up, looking down at her and grinning. "That feather thing is pretty sexy, even if it is a cat toy. Want to see how it feels?"

She grinned back. "Are you going to tie me to the bed?"

"Do you want to be tied?"

"I think I do, but maybe we should have some rules for how we proceed."

"Agreed. Now what else do you have in that bag of tricks you bought?"

"Like you said, we've got time to find out."

"The rest of our lives," he answered. He had never felt happier in his life, never more grounded, never more content. With his lifemate at his side, everything had changed. In ways he was only beginning to understand.

DECORAH SECURITY SERIES
(sexy paranormal romantic suspense)
BY REBECCA YORK

#1. ON EDGE (e-book novella and Decorah prequel).
#2. DARK MOON (e-book and trade paperback novel).
#3. CHAINED (e-book novella).
#4. AMBUSHED (e-book short story).
#5. DARK POWERS (e-book and trade paperback novel).
#6. HOT AND DANGEROUS (e-book short story).
#7. AT RISK (e-book and trade paperback novel).
#8. CHRISTMAS CAPTIVE (e-book novella).
#9. DESTINATION WEDDING (e-book novella).
#10. RX MISSING (e-book novel)

DECORAH SECURITY COLLECTION (e-book including *Ambushed, Hot and Dangerous, Chained,* and *Dark Powers*).

OFF-WORLD SERIES
(sexy science-fiction romance)
BY REBECCA YORK

#1. ON EDGE (e-book novella and Decorah prequel).
#2. HERO'S WELCOME (e-book romance short story).
#3. CONQUEST (e-book romance short story).
#4. ASSIGNMENT DANGER (e-book romance novella).
#5. CHRISTMAS HOME (e-book romance short story).

OFF WORLD COLLECTION (e-book including *Nightfall, Hero's Welcome,* and *Conquest*).

PRAISE FOR REBECCA YORK

Rebecca York delivers page-turning suspense.
—Nora Roberts

Rebecca York never fails to deliver. Her strong characterizations, imaginative plots and sensuous love scenes have made fans of thousands of romance, romantic suspense and thriller readers.
—Chassie West

Rebecca York will thrill you with romance, kill you with danger and chill you with the supernatural.
—Patricia Rosemoor

(Rebecca York) is a real luminary of contemporary series romance
—Michael Dirda, The Washington Post Book World

Rebecca York's writing is fast-paced, suspenseful, and loaded with tension.
—Jayne Ann Krentz

ABOUT REBECCA YORK

A New York Times and USA Today best-Selling author, Rebecca York is one of fewer than 20 romance novelists ever to receive the Romance Writers of America Centennial Award for having written over 100 romance novels. Her career has focused on romantic suspense, often with paranormal elements.

Her 16 Berkley books and novellas include her nine-book werewolf "Moon" series. KILLING MOON was a launch book for the Berkley Sensation imprint. She has written 75 books for Harlequin, many in her popular 43 Light Street series for Harlequin Intrigue. She has written for Harlequin, Berkley, Sourcebooks, Dell, Tor, Carina Press, and Pageant Books.

As Ruth Glick, Rebecca has also published sixteen cookbooks, one of which (100 PERCENT PLEASURE, with Nancy Baggett) was picked by USA Today as one of the twelve best cookbooks of 1994. Her most recent cookbook is THE 2 DAY A WEEK DIET COOKBOOK, available as both an e-book and trade paperback.

Her many awards include two Rita finalist books. She has two Career Achievement awards from Romantic Times: for Series Romantic Suspense and for Series Romantic Mystery. And her Peregrine Connection series won a Lifetime Achievement Award for Romantic Suspense Series.

Many of her novels have been nominated for or won RT Reviewers Choice awards. In addition, she has won a Prism Award, several New Jersey Romance Writers Golden Leaf awards and numerous other chapter awards.

Web site: www.RebeccaYork.com
E-mail: rebecca@rebeccayork.com
Facebook: www.facebook.com/ruthglick
Twitter: @rebeccayork43
Blog: www.rebeccayork.blogspot.com

CPSIA information can be obtained
at www.ICGtesting.com
Printed in the USA
BVOW06s1942120117
473360BV00016B/193/P